MW01442003

Baker College of Flint Library

PROPERTY OF
Baker College of

CRIMINAL INVESTIGATIONS

CONS AND FRAUDS

CRIMINAL INVESTIGATIONS

Bank Robbery
Celebrities and Crime
Child Abduction and Kidnapping
Cons and Frauds
Crime Scene Investigation
Cybercrime
Drug Crime
Gangs and Gang Crime
Homicide
Organized Crime
Serial Killers
Terrorism
Unsolved Crimes
White-Collar Crime

CRIMINAL INVESTIGATIONS

CONS AND FRAUDS

MICHAEL BENSON

Consulting Editor: JOHN L. FRENCH,
CRIME SCENE SUPERVISOR,
BALTIMORE POLICE CRIME LABORATORY

CHELSEA HOUSE
PUBLISHERS
An imprint of Infobase Publishing

CRIMINAL INVESTIGATIONS: Cons and Frauds

Copyright © 2009 by Infobase Publishing

All rights reserved. No part of this book may be reproduced or utilized in any form or by any means, electronic or mechanical, including photocopying, recording, or by any information storage or retrieval systems, without permission in writing from the publisher. For information contact:

Chelsea House
An imprint of Infobase Publishing
132 West 31st Street
New York NY 10001

Library of Congress Cataloging-in-Publication Data
Benson, Michael.
Cons and frauds / Michael Benson ; consulting editor, John L. French.
 p. cm. — (Criminal investigations)
Includes bibliographical references and index.
ISBN-13: 978-0-7910-9404-4 (alk. paper)
ISBN-10: 0-7910-9404-9 (alk. paper)
1. Swindlers and swindling. 2. Fraud. 3. Fraud—Prevention. I. French, John L. II. Title. III. Series.
HV6691.B46 2008   364.16′3—dc22
             2008019148

Chelsea House books are available at special discounts when purchased in bulk quantities for businesses, associations, institutions, or sales promotions. Please call our Special Sales Department in New York at (212) 967-8800 or (800) 322-8755.

You can find Chelsea House on the World Wide Web at
http://www.chelseahouse.com

Text design by Erika K. Arroyo
Cover design by Ben Peterson

Cover: Con artists sometimes bribe public officials or organized crime figures so their scams can go unpunished.

Printed in the United States of America

Bang EJB 10 9 8 7 6 5 4 3 2 1

This book is printed on acid-free paper.

All links and Web addresses were checked and verified to be correct at the time of publication. Because of the dynamic nature of the Web, some addresses and links may have changed since publication and may no longer be valid.

*To the sucker who, being born every minute,
is getting pretty tired of it.*

◆

Contents

Foreword	9
Acknowledgments	13
Introduction	15
1 Using the Mark's Greed: Types of Cons	19
2 Anatomy of a Con	29
3 The Impersonator	35
4 Common Scams	43
5 ID Theft	57
6 E-Cons: Scamming on the Grifter Superhighway	63
7 World Without Shame	73
8 Public Education and Protection Against Cons	79
9 Media Investigations: *60 Minutes*	87
Chronology	95
Endnotes	97
Glossary	102
Bibliography	103
Further Resources	105
Index	106
About the Author	111
About the Consulting Editor	112

Foreword

In 2000 there were 15,000 murders in the United States. During that same year about a half million people were assaulted, 1.1 million cars were stolen, 400,000 robberies took place, and more than 2 million homes and businesses were broken into. All told, in the last year of the twentieth century, there were more than 11 million crimes committed in this country.*

In 2000 the population of the United States was approximately 280 million people. If each of the above crimes happened to a separate person, only 4 percent of the country would have been directly affected. Yet everyone is in some way affected by crime. Taxes pay patrolmen, detectives, and scientists to investigate it, lawyers and judges to prosecute it, and correctional officers to watch over those convicted of committing it. Crimes against businesses cause prices to rise as their owners pass on the cost of theft and security measures installed to prevent future losses. Tourism in cities, and the money it brings in, may rise and fall in part due to stories about crime in their streets. And every time someone is shot, stabbed, beaten, or assaulted, or when someone is jailed for having committed such a crime, not only they suffer but so may their friends, family, and loved ones. Crime affects everyone.

It is the job of the police to investigate crime with the purpose of putting the bad guys in jail and keeping them there, hoping thereby to punish past crimes and discourage new ones. To accomplish this a police officer has to be many things: dedicated, brave, smart, honest, and imaginative. Luck helps, but it's not required. And there's one more virtue that should be associated with law enforcement. A good police officer is patient.

10 CONS AND FRAUDS

Patience is a virtue in crime fighting because police officers and detectives know something that most criminals don't. It's not a secret, but most lawbreakers don't learn it until it is too late. Criminals who make money robbing people, breaking into houses, or stealing cars; who live by dealing drugs or committing murder; who spend their days on the wrong side of the law, or commit any other crimes, must remember this: a criminal has to get away with every crime he or she commits. However, to get criminals off the street and put them behind bars, the police only have to catch a criminal once.

The methods by which police catch criminals are varied. Some are as old as recorded history and others are so new that they have yet to be tested in court. One of the first stories in the Bible is of murder, when Cain killed his brother Abel (Genesis 4:1–16). With few suspects to consider and an omniscient detective, this was an easy crime to solve. However, much later in that same work, a young man named Daniel steps in when a woman is accused of an immoral act by two elders (Daniel 13:1–63). By using the standard police practice of separating the witnesses before questioning them, he is able to arrive at the truth of the matter.

From the time of the Bible to almost present day, police investigations did not progress much further than questioning witnesses and searching the crime scene for obvious clues as to a criminal's identity. It was not until the late 1800s that science began to be employed. In 1879 the French began to use physical measurements and later photography to identify repeat offenders. In the same year a Scottish missionary in Japan used a handprint found on a wall to exonerate a man accused of theft. In 1892 a bloody fingerprint led Argentine police to charge and convict a mother of killing her children, and by 1905 Scotland Yard had convicted several criminals thanks to this new science.

Progress continued. By the 1920s scientists were using blood analysis to determine if recovered stains were from the victim or suspect, and the new field of firearms examination helped link bullets to the guns that fired them.

Nowadays, things are even harder on criminals, when by leaving behind a speck of blood, dropping a sweat-stained hat, or even taking a sip from a can of soda, they can give the police everything they need to identify and arrest them.

In the first decade of the twenty-first century the main tools used by the police include

- questioning witnesses and suspects
- searching the crime scene for physical evidence
- employing informants and undercover agents
- investigating the whereabouts of previous offenders when a crime they've been known to commit has occurred
- using computer databases to match evidence found on one crime scene to that found on others or to previously arrested suspects
- sharing information with other law enforcement agencies via the Internet
- using modern communications to keep the public informed and enlist their aid in ongoing investigations

But just as they have many different tools with which to solve crime, so too do they have many different kinds of crime and criminals to investigate. There is murder, kidnapping, and bank robbery. There are financial crimes committed by con men who gain their victim's trust or computer experts who hack into computers. There are criminals who have formed themselves into gangs and those who are organized into national syndicates. And there are those who would kill as many people as possible, either for the thrill of taking a human life or in the horribly misguided belief that it will advance their cause.

The Criminal Investigations series looks at all of the above and more. Each book in the series takes one type of crime and gives the reader an overview of the history of the crime, the methods and motives behind it, the people who have committed it, and the means by which these people are caught and punished. In this series celebrity crimes will be discussed and exposed. Mysteries that have yet to be solved will be presented. Readers will discover the truth about murderers, serial killers, and bank robbers whose stories have become myths and legends. These books will explain how criminals can separate a person from his hard-earned cash, how they prey on the weak and helpless, what is being done to stop them, and what one can do to help prevent becoming a victim.

John L. French,
Crime Scene Supervisor,
Baltimore Police Crime Laboratory

* Federal Bureau of Investigation. "Uniform Crime Reports, Crime in the United States 2000." Available online. URL: http://www.fbi.gov/ucr/00cius.htm. Accessed January 11, 2008.

Acknowledgments

The author would like to gratefully acknowledge all of the persons who helped in the production of this book. Without their help it would have been impossible. Editor James Chambers, my agent Jake Elwell, private investigator Vincent Parco, my wife Lisa Grasso, author David Henry Jacobs, former NYPD Cop of the Year and all-around good guy Robert Mladinich, Philip Semrau, Nathan Versace, Keith Brenner, Eddie and Cate Behringer, Larry Beck, and Scott Frommer.

Introduction

Some criminals use violence—or the threat of violence—to part their victims from their money. Other criminals use their gift for gab, and some lie or deceive, to steal. These criminals are known as confidence men (or women), con artists, or **grifters**.

When a con artist is on top of his game, the money is not even taken against the victim's will. The victim—or **mark**, as he is referred to by those committing the crime—gives the money willingly to the crook. Only later does he realize that he has been given empty promises, that his money, and the con man, are gone forever.

It has been estimated that more money is made each year through confidence games and frauds than through all other forms of professional crime combined.[1] It is hard to estimate a dollar figure because con-game victims are unlikely to report the crime.

There are a few reasons for this. The mark may not only be embarrassed by what has occurred, but also may fear the police. A successful con sometimes involves the mark doing something illegal before he is robbed. He can't tell the police that his money was stolen without admitting to breaking the law himself. Con artists exploit the dishonesty of their marks. If a mark has broken the law, the police and the district attorney would have to grant the victim immunity from prosecution for his crimes if they were to have any chance of getting him to testify against a con artist.

The victim might also feel anxious that the con artist is part of a larger, organized group—mobsters or the Mafia—that might seek revenge if it felt wronged by the victim's blabbermouth.

Even when the mark is innocent, he may still be reluctant to come forward and admit he was taken. Being fleeced by a professional con artist makes the victim feel stupid. Marks might want to keep the facts of the case to themselves for the simple reason that they fear the embarrassment of anyone else finding out it happened. Bottom line: Many are ripped off. Few go to the cops.[2]

According to con expert Patricia H. Holmes, "Consumers of any age can become victims of a con artist. Older adults who become victims of fraud may experience feelings of hurt, anger, grief, loss, guilt, betrayal, or embarrassment. These feelings can be used constructively to keep you, a friend, or a family member from becoming a victim of consumer fraud. Remember, if something sounds too good to be true, it probably is."[3]

The good news is people can protect themselves. This book is packed with information about how con games work, and how to keep from becoming a mark. There are three quick rules of thumb to follow whenever dealing with money, and especially when dealing with *strangers* and money. They are:

1. Ask questions before making a decision.
2. Don't be pressured into a quick decision.
3. Talk to a friend or relative before making a decision.

Con artists do not want their marks to carefully consider their proposals. They rely on getting victims to trust them and make a quick decision. And remember, con artists approach their marks in many different ways. They may contact them in person, striking up a casual conversation. They may call on the phone or send e-mail.

In general, avoid being overly trusting of strangers. Avoid giving strangers the benefit of the doubt or thinking things like, "No one would be so underhanded." They *would*, and they *will*. This book will explain how to avoid being swindled, and what those who *are* cheated by a con artist can do about it.[4]

This book will also look at the ways in which law enforcement has gone about stopping con artists, and the difficulties police have in bringing con artists to justice.

In legal terms, most con games are referred to as *fraud*. Thus, the fraud department of the police force fights this type of crime. For years, that department has had a common nickname: the **bunco** squad.

Bunco squad is a term that some people might remember from old movies and television shows. The name came from the dice game called *Bunco*, which was almost always used for gambling, and which was frequently rigged. Eventually, *bunco* became a generic term for anything pertaining to swindling or fraud of any kind. The term has even been used as a verb, as in the stage musical *Oklahoma!* in which one character exclaims, "Say, young feller, you certainly bunkoed me!"[5]

The original bunco game was a variation of a Spanish card game called *banco*. The word first came to mean a generic swindle in the United States in the years following the Civil War. The first official bunco squads, teams of law enforcement personnel working to stop confidence games, were formed during the 1940s. Many cops who work the modern-day bunco beat are pretty good at deception themselves. Luckily for the world they have decided to channel this skill in a positive direction.

When a con job is reported, the bunco squad may gather evidence against the criminals by using an undercover agent. In other words, the police provide the criminal with a mark, one who is wearing modern surveillance equipment.

The undercover agent—also known as a mole—only pretends to be a mark. He allows himself to be swindled by the criminals while transmitting crucial evidence back to the investigators. When everything goes well, cops can rush in and arrests can be made on the spot.

Another method the bunco squad uses is the informant. An informant is someone inside a criminal organization, or with knowledge of that organization, who tells police what they know. Usually, this method is used to break up a larger operation after one, sometimes small, figure in the operation has been arrested.

The criminal is offered a deal by the police: usually a lesser sentence or no jail time in exchange for gathering information and testifying against other members of the operation. Desperate to keep jail time to a minimum, the arrested criminal blabs everything he knows. Sometimes he agrees to wear a wire, that is, return to his gang with a microphone or camera, perhaps disguised as a button, hidden on his person.

Using the microphone, police can record the con artists talking about the crimes they have committed. In some cases, the informant may be able to gather evidence of swindles as they are taking place.

Still, since so few confidence games are reported, the bunco squad's effort to arrest con artists is often unsuccessful. By far the most successful method of hindering con games, police have found, is to educate the public. If the public knows how the scams work, they are less likely to become marks.

Con artists have kept up with modern technology and use the Internet in many of their current scams. The bunco squads have stayed modern, as well. They are experts at searching the Internet for online con games.

The concept of con games is sometimes best explained through comedy. Cons are a very popular subject in film. That was certainly the case with *You Can't Cheat an Honest Man*, a 1939 comedy classic starring and written by W.C. Fields. In this film, Fields plays Larsen E. Whipsnade, the owner of a shady carnival that is constantly on the run from the law. The title derives from an earlier Fields film in which he says that his grandfather's last words were, "You can't cheat an honest man; never give a sucker an even break, or smarten up a chump."[6] Some of the most popular movies about con artists will be discussed throughout this book.

Using the Mark's Greed:
Types of Cons

You're the con artist, and this is your scam: You convince your mark that you have built a machine that prints $20 bills. You even give your hapless victim a demonstration. Turn the crank and, sure enough, real money comes out of a slot.

The mark agrees to buy a machine for $100,000, with the first $25,000 expected in advance. The mark believes the machine will pay for itself in days. Of course, once he gets the machine home he finds he has purchased a fake. The demonstration was a trick and he's out $25,000. The mark's greed was so intense that he never saw the deception coming.[1]

Con artists use the mark's greed against him. Many cons are a simple variation of the old "money box" scam, which has been around for as long as there has been paper money.

RICO LAWS

In recent years, the U.S. Congress has passed laws making con artists easier to arrest, try, and convict. Using these laws, the government can better combat groups of criminals working together to commit crimes, as is sometimes the case in confidence operations.

The most effective of these laws have been the so-called RICO Laws. RICO stands for the Racketeer Influenced and Corrupt

Organizations Act. It is suspected that the name was chosen because a character named Rico was the big cheese in an old-time gangster movie called *Little Caesar*, which was was one of the all-time favorite movies of G. Robert Blakey, the author of the RICO laws.[2]

The RICO Laws were passed by Congress in the fall of 1970. They allowed law enforcement to arrest criminals who conspired with others to profit from an illegal business, a crime called racketeering. If a crook was part of a group that was committing a crime and helped that group in any way commit the crime, he was guilty of committing the crime. The laws against racketeering became a new weapon against the racket of confidence games. They also allowed people who had lost money because of a con game to sue the con artist to get their money back in triplicate.[3]

SILENT MARKS

If con men are experts at anything it is at getting away with their crimes. They not only rely on bribes that prevent law enforcement from properly controlling their activities, but they make sure their victims never tell the police that they have been robbed.

JAMES WHITAKER WRIGHT

One of the first known con men to work on a grand scale, and earn a fortune in the process, was James Whitaker Wright (1845–1904). Originally from England, as a young man he lived in Philadelphia, where he made millions selling silver mines out west.

The properties he sold usually existed, but not once did the "mine" turn out to have any silver in it. He returned to England with his fortune before law enforcement caught up with him. In 1904 he was convicted of fraud and sentenced to seven years in prison. He killed himself rather than serve his time behind bars.[4]

Many years later, James Whitaker Wright III, a grandson of the original, developed a BBC One television show called *Hustle*, about confidence games and how they work; it premiered in May 2006 and has been a hit since.[5] Today, mining certificates signed by Wright are worth hundreds of dollars as memorabilia, as a tribute to a more gullible time.[6]

Making the mark think that he or she is in on a scam is one way of controlling the mark after the swindle. The mark will be unwilling to tell the police that he was swindled because he thought he was going to make a large sum of money illegally. Another way con artists keep marks' mouths shut is to run their operations in conjunction with other illegal activities. For example, a scam may be run out of a house of prostitution. The mark, after being swindled, cannot report the crime without making an embarrassing admission. Another scam, the **button**, has the con artist arrested by a phony cop, who allows the mark to talk his way out of being taken into custody, thus ensuring his or her silence.

SHORT CONS

Before delving into more complex con games, it is helpful to take a look at some of the most simple. In some cases the con artist can find, set up, and swindle a victim, then get away, all in a short period of time. This is a short con, or little con.

Short cons tend to be quick, and victims are easy to find. One of the key differences between a short con and a big con is that, with the short version, the mark is never sent home to get more money.

One common short con is best known as "short-changing." The criminal routinely miscounts and exchanges money to his benefit. One trick is to pay for an item with a large bill, and then substitute a smaller bill at the last second. In modern times, most cashiers in stores carefully count the money they are given and the money they return to the shopper to make sure they are not being short-changed by a con artist.

Another common form of short con is the shell game. This scam has the advantage of giving the criminal the ability to rip off many marks all at one location. The criminal sets up a table on a busy street. Two assistants stand with him, pretending to be strangers. These assistants are **shills**, or **inside men**.

When a likely customer walks by, one of the shills says something like, "You got to play this game. This idiot is giving away money."

"Say what?" says the mark.

"There's a pea under one of his three shells and he thinks he's good at confusing you, but he's no good at it. I just took $500 off him."

CONS AND FRAUDS

A variation of the shell game, a common form of short con. *Lawrence Manning/Corbis*

Filled with confidence, the mark puts his money down and bets that he will be able to tell, after the shells have been moved around for a spell, which shell covers the pea. He may be allowed to win a couple of small wagers at first, just to draw him further into the game. But, as soon as the wagers become large, the mark's luck runs out. The mark loses his money.

Confidence is the name of the game. These are called confidence games because the idea is to make the mark confident—even overconfident—that he cannot lose. That way, the mark bets much more than he would if he were gambling at a legitimate game.

If the mark thinks losing must be a fluke, one of the shills might say, "Go ahead, give it another try. You're bound to get it right this time."

Using the Mark's Greed

"Oh, all right," the mark says and plops down his money.

Again he loses. Dejected, he leaves, and another mark is recruited.

The operation can stay in one place for a long time before a beat cop strolls by or someone complains about getting ripped off. The small table, three shells, and the pea are easy to pick up and run with.

The shell game does not have to be played with shells and a pea. It can be played with three cards, one of which is a queen. The cards have been folded down the center, so the artist can move them around swiftly. The mark is asked to pick which card is the queen, and he's always right until he bets it all. Then he is taken and told to move along, sometimes under threat of violence if he protests. This card game is known as Three-Card Monte, or sometimes Find the Lady.[7]

A common con game 50 years ago was **tat**. It was basically a dice game with fixed dice. The con artist used a peculiar pair of dice. One die was normal with the normal number of spots on each side. The other had five dots on four sides and six dots on the other two sides.

This con usually involved two men and occurred most frequently in bars, where marks had been drinking and several marks could be taken at once. One man is the roper, and he attracts the mark into the game. The other is a shill.

The roper gets a bunch of men together along a bar or at a table. He tells them that he has recently learned this bar game and it's a lot of fun, and easy. He then accidentally drops one of his dice on the floor, giving one of the players a chance to examine the die and see that it is legit. The roper puts the legit die in his pocket. If someone asks about this, he says that only one die is needed to play the game, but in most cases no one says anything. They are thinking in terms of having fun and eagerly hand the roper their money. Among those playing is the inside man.

"First, I take money from each of you. Then we each roll the dice three times. The one with the highest total gets everybody's money." The roper appoints one of the marks to be the "official scorekeeper."

The game is played with the legitimate die until the marks are more drunk. Then the roper suggests upping the ante.

Instead of putting dollars in the pot, they should put twenties into the pot. A few of the players might drop out at this point, saying the game has become "too rich for their blood," but most agree to continue playing.

Once the stakes have risen, the inside man's luck becomes hot and he wins every round. That's because the marks are throwing the legit die while the inside man rolls the die that is nothing but fives and sixes.

When the marks have been fleeced of their money, the roper ends the game and splits. The inside man, rosy-cheeked over his luck, buys a round and then calls it a night himself. The marks head home with empty wallets and usually don't even know they have been swindled.

BIG CONS

The big con, sometimes called the long con, takes more time and effort than a short con—but the payoff for the criminal is usually larger. Short cons can victimize just about anyone, someone off the street or the people who happen to be sitting at the bar—as long as they have a few bucks in their pocket. Short cons put the bite on a mark for the money he has on him. Big cons target the rich and try to fleece from the mark every dime he has, plus his house and his car.

In many cases, the big con comes with its own place of business, which is almost like a movie set, designed to give the mark confidence and make him believe. If the con involves a stock-market theme, a suite of offices may be rented and decorated to resemble the real thing.

If a mobster-wannabe is the mark, a storefront may be rented, the window painted black, and the insides decorated like an Italian-American "social club," with an espresso machine behind a bar, an old TV showing European soccer, and a couple of slot machines in the back.

In the language of the con, this setting—the phony place designed to separate the mark from his money—is called the big store.

One common big con is the **rag**, and it involves the stock market. A mark, who preferred to remain nameless, first reported about the rag:

Using the Mark's Greed

I used to be a big gambler. I loved to play poker and go to the racetrack and bet on the ponies, but one form of gambling I learned to lay off right away was the stock market. Maybe if I'd have had more success up front I might have stayed in

THE STING

An excellent example of a big con can be found in the Academy Award winning movie *The Sting*, which came out in 1973 and starred Paul Newman and Robert Redford. When a mob boss kills their mutual friend, Newman and Redford get even by conning the boss out of a fortune. They do this by convincing the mobster that they have an off-track betting establishment that supposedly knows the results of horse races before those results arrive via telegraph. Their establishment is totally make believe. There are several twists and turns in the plot (which won't be revealed here), but the brilliant script is written so that both the audience and the mobster are conned!

Robert Shaw, Robert Redford, and Paul Newman in *The Sting*. Sunset Boulevard/Corbis

26 CONS AND FRAUDS

it longer. But to say that my luck in the stock market was a little chilly would be an understatement. A guy came to me one day, this was many years ago, and he told me that he'd bought a stock at twenty-five cents a share. He bought it on account of his cleaning lady's aunt worked at the place and had the inside scoop, knowledge of what was going on days before it was announced to the public. It went up to three dollars two days later. Boom, he's in the money. The guy says to me, 'You got to get in on this and you got to get in on this right away because this stock is going up to twenty dollars.' The stock was a Filipino gold mine. The rumor was that they had just struck a new vein of gold. It was like striking oil. So I went to the bank and I took out $3,000. I swear to my mother, this is a true story. I gave the money to the guy and I said, 'Buy me a thousand shares at three bucks a share. You can put the shares under your name. I trust you.' I swear to you, the next day, the very next day, the stock dropped to seven cents a share. That was it for the stock market for me.[8]

And that was just a small example of the scam. How much of the con artist's story is true depends on the scam. In the above example, maybe the Filipino gold mine actually existed, maybe it didn't. The only thing that mattered was that the con artist took the mark's money. The rag usually involves the stock market, and, in more complex schemes, the mark actually makes a small profit with his first few investments. Only when he "bets it all" does the stock tank and the con artist walk away with all the money.

In some cases, millionaires are wiped out as they think have inside knowledge that will—illegally—make them a fortune. This is referred to as insider trading. But because the mark of this kind of big con knows that insider trading is illegal, he is less likely to report the con once he becomes aware of it.

For example, a mark is steered to fake stockbroker offices. The brokerage has an inside **tip**—a more sophisticated version of the "cleaning-lady's-aunt-works-there" story. Somebody knows somebody who works in the foreign embassy of a fictional land (say, the country of Moronica) and they're about to declare war on a neighboring nation. Everybody in the country is going to need a gun. They push the con to invest in guns manufactured in that country. Perhaps phony brochures have been printed. There may even be a special telephone line set up so that, if the mark calls the company to make sure it is real, he will get a receptionist saying "Moronica Guns, may I help you?"

The rag, like all successful cons, exploits human nature. Businessmen don't like to gamble as a rule. They like "sure things": moneymaking schemes in which "the fix is in." By providing a temptation that feeds into that desire, the con artist usually has little trouble finding marks willing to empty their wallets (and bank accounts) in the hopes of making "free money."

Anatomy of a Con

A con **job** is sometimes complicated, but all cons have a similar structure: a beginning, middle, and an end. This chapter follows a con artist working through the stages of a con, examining it piece by piece to better understand how it works. Almost all con jobs follow the same pattern from beginning to conclusion.

PUTTING THE MARK UP

Locating a victim is called "putting the mark up." That's your first task. In choosing a mark, you have a short checklist you run through. How rich is the mark? How easily is he fooled? You're in it for the money, so you look for signs of wealth first. The location of the first contact is often geared to weed out poor people. (You are more apt to work a country club than a soup kitchen.) The mark should not only be rich, but also a person who loves to spend money.

You are a member of a confidence-game team, and as the middle man, your job is to recruit marks. You are looking for marks who are busy living life. The hangar for private planes is a good place to make first contact. Yacht clubs are also popular hunting grounds.

PLAYING THE CON AND ROPING THE MARK

This step involves earning the mark's trust. The con artist becomes a quick friend to the mark. Good con artists do their homework. If you are recruiting marks at a yacht club, you will know the difference between a keelboat and a catamaran. You will know the captain of the sailboat who won the last America's Cup competition.

And, you must look the part. You will have a tan. Your clothes will be appropriate for that setting. You'll know which shoes to wear and the appropriate drink to order at the bar. You are an actor, and you must play your part well. Any mistake, or **bobble**, can tip off the mark and spoil the con.

You must also be patient. Once you have chosen your mark, you must befriend him at a reasonable pace. You will do a couple of favors for the mark; ask for his advice. By the time the con begins, the mark must trust you completely and no longer think of you as a stranger. Once that trust is gained, you lead the mark to the inside man, who will carry on the con from there. When the middle man leads the mark to the inside man, it is called "roping the mark."

TELLING THE TALE

You have prepared your mark well for his meeting with the inside man. Say, for example, your con game has to do with phony stocks. You have told the mark that your broker (the inside man) has inside

DIDDLING

One of the first American writers to expose the nature of con games in his work was Edgar Allan Poe, who wrote about various cons and scams in his story "Diddling Considered as one of the Exact Sciences."[1] Diddling, in essence, involves a con artist selling something that doesn't belong to him. In Poe's classic example, a woman who is shopping for a sofa happens upon a furniture warehouse where a man, standing outside the door, tells her that the furniture inside is 20 percent off. He takes her inside, allows her to pick out the sofa she likes, takes her money, and promises to deliver the sofa that afternoon. Of course, the sofa never shows up. When the woman returns to complain, she learns that the salesman who "took care of her" doesn't work at the warehouse. No one even knows who he is. A con man happened upon an unattended warehouse and took the opportunity to scam the woman.

knowledge of the stock market. He knows ahead of time which stocks are going to skyrocket in value and which ones will plummet in worth. By the time the mark meets the inside man, he is primed and ready to pull out his wallet.

The inside man explains the moneymaking scheme that will make the mark richer than his wildest dreams. The tale may have several variations depending on the scruples of the mark. The mark makes a small investment, just for a taste of the action.

GIVING THE MARK THE CONVINCER

Confidence games involve patience at every step. You can't expect your mark to empty his bank account right away. First, you have to convince him that the scam is "real." This is "the convincer" or "the **blow**."

Here, the con artist allows the mark to make money back, promising there is a lot more where that came from. Of course, this money does not come out of the con artist's pocket. It is merely a percentage of the very money the mark has already invested in the scam. In this case, the mark's first investment using the broker's advice earns him an immediate dividend. The amount of payback varies depending on the scam's eventual payoff. During the early stages of a con, some inside men like to give the mark back more money than he gave, so the mark has made a profit. This further convinces the mark that the scam is real, hooking him good. Of course, at the end of the scam, the mark loses all of his money in the final fleece.

One of the ways you convince the mark that your broker is real is to create a believable setting. Teams of con artists will rent an office and furnish it and decorate it so that it looks like a real brokerage firm down to the smallest detail.

GIVING THE BREAKDOWN

Once you have your mark convinced that your brokerage is real, it is time to take all of his money. If the fellow has $1 million in the bank, tell him that you can turn that into $5 million in less than a week. Then send him to the bank to get the money.

32 CONS AND FRAUDS

TAKING OFF THE TOUCH

This is the step where the con man executes the scam and takes the mark's money. Your mark has returned from the bank with the money and hands it over. You assure him that he has done the right thing. You say you have some other business to take care of, but you'll see him later back at the yacht club for a drink.

After the completion of a long con, con artists often dismantle the fake office they constructed and relocate to find a new mark. *Berthold Litjes/zefa/Corbis*

BLOWING HIM OFF

With the mark's money in hand, the con man gets away from the mark with as little fuss as possible. He will not meet his mark later at the yacht club for a drink. In fact, if he can help it, the con man will never see the mark again. He will be too busy dismantling the office he constructed and moving it to a new location, where he will find a new mark and start the scam all over again.

PUTTING IN THE FIX

There are two primary concerns when you are a con artist. The first, of course, is to get the money. The second is to not get caught. The final step in a scam is "putting in the **fix**," which means preventing law enforcement involvement. This can be done either by, as was true in this case, moving the place of operation after every con, or by bribing the police to look the other way.[2] If the mark has taken part in illegal activity as part of the

---

KAYFABE: LANGUAGE OF THE CON

The swindle was such an integral part of traveling carnivals in the early to mid-twentieth century that carneys—those who worked for the carnival—developed their own language for it. It was called **kayfabe**. Loosely translated, *kayfabe* meant talking in front of the mark about the con, without the mark realizing it—or staying in character.

Kayfabe might have died out, along with the traveling carnival, except it was adopted by the pro wrestling racket. The spectacle of wrestling, not to be confused with traditional, competitive wrestling, was an outgrowth of the carnival, where traveling wrestlers took on all comers and worked the same scam in town after town, wrestling accomplices planted in the crowd and getting away with it.

Even after pro wrestling became a televised sport, the use of kayfabe by its participants continued. Right up until the 1980s, professional wrestling portrayed itself as actual competition when in reality the matches were pre-scripted.

con, it's even less likely that he'll go to the cops, for fear of implicating himself.

Cons all work alike. They vary, however, in how cruel they are. When a con artist rips off a greedy rich person, eager himself to make money he didn't earn, it almost seems like the mark had it coming. It is more difficult for most people to forgive con artists who rip off the innocent. Sometimes, in addition to being innocent, the marks are frightened and desperate, making the grifter who rips them off all that much more despicable.

The Impersonator

All con artists have good acting skills. Grifters are always pretending to be someone or something that they are not. When con artists pretend to be salesmen, the product they are selling frequently turns out to be phony as well.

The prize-winning Broadway musical (and later movie) *The Music Man* is about a traveler who pretends he is a bandleader. He came to small towns, convincing the townspeople that their youth would become criminals unless they found something good and wholesome to occupy their time. The cure, he would say, was a band, a musical band, which he would teach and direct. When the townspeople paid—in advance, of course—for the band's instruments and uniforms, the con man would slip out of town with the money.

OFFICER IMPOSTOR

Although modern communications have wiped out the traveling con artist who rips off entire towns at once, impersonation remains a common con technique. Impersonation, pretending to be someone you're not, works best when the created character is someone easy to trust.

Con men pretend to be priests, firefighters, doctors—the very people their marks are most apt to take at their word. For example, in 2007 a man pretending to be a policeman cheated citizens in Long Island, New York. This con artist's act was so complete that even his roommate did not know that he wasn't a law-enforcement officer. The con's name was Henry Terry and he was, in reality, an unemployed 25-year-old on probation for arson.[1]

36 CONS AND FRAUDS

Terry made the most of pretending he was a cop. He had a uniform, a badge, a gun, handcuffs, and all of the equipment one would associate with law enforcement. He wore a bulletproof vest. He had a clipboard with official-looking forms clamped to it. He filled

This police poster shows Henry Terry with some of the props he used while posing as a police officer. *AP Photo*

out "an official report" while interviewing persons he had caught "breaking the law."

His biggest prop was his car. Terry drove a late-model Ford Crown Victoria with a siren light on top and a loudspeaker for pulling drivers over. He later said that he got all of his police equipment on the Internet.

Con artists feel no remorse—no matter how shameful they behave. So Terry made sure he sewed a 9/11 commemorative patch to the shoulder of his bogus police uniform. If there were no speeders, he could always collect money for a fake 9/11 relief fund.

For years he made a living by taking bribes, pulling over speeders, and saving drivers the trip to court by fining them and taking their money right there at the side of the road. Sometimes he would shake down prostitutes and their clients, taking their money in exchange for not arresting them.

Terry completely fooled his friends and neighbors. That done, it was easy to fool the marks, many of whom were frightened and embarrassed at being caught breaking the law. Terry did actual police work, found actual people committing crimes, and got money from them. In exchange, he "let them go."[2]

"He had the kids idolizing him like he was a super police officer," said one of his neighbors. "He would come out in his uniform every day, like he was going to work. He would flash his lights for the kids. He would let them play with the siren."[3]

Terry didn't always tell people the same story. Sometimes he said he was a police officer. He told others he was a police sergeant. Sometimes he was a county cop, and sometimes he worked for the state. In plain clothes, he might tell a mark that he was a special agent with the FBI.

Terry might have been able to continue his scams for years, but he got greedy. He tried a new scam. On two occasions he got citizens, individuals he'd never seen before, to give him their motor vehicles.

In the first instance, he told a man that he needed to take his Hummer for "police work." When the fellow hesitated, as expected, Terry told him that the state would pay him back double for the vehicle and gave the mark a bogus business card. The mark handed him the keys.

CONS FOR FUN

Con artists have been known to love the games they play so much that they have pulled cons just for laughs. One favorite fun scam occurs when a young man and an old man are working as a team.

The old man will appear passed out on a barstool in an all-but-deserted bar, his wallet sticking three-quarters out of his pocket. The young man will enter the bar accompanied by a young lady who he has recently met.

They are early in a relationship and she is unaware of how the young man makes a living. The couple sits in a booth and the young man says, "Hey, look at that old drunk, his wallet is practically falling out of his pocket. I dare you to pick his pocket."

Soon, possibly after a little encouragement, the young woman picks the pocket and the two skedaddle into the night. When they get to their next stop, usually another bar down the street, the woman checks the wallet to see how much money she made. This scam has a couple of endings:

1. The wallet is thick, but she opens the wallet to find that there is no money, just sheet after sheet of blank paper, some of which might have dirty poems written on them.
2. The money is real, but as the young woman is counting it, the "old drunk," now sober and alert, enters the bar where the young man and his date are "hiding" and demands his wallet back.

    Sometimes the girl catches on right away and this is how she learns what her boyfriend does for a living. Sometimes the young woman makes a run for it, thinking she has just been caught "stealing." Either way, the two-man team of con artists enjoy a good laugh at the mark's expense.

In the second instance, he told a mark that he needed his Toyota Land Rover for an FBI investigation. Again, the mark turned over the keys. But this mark quickly became suspicious and reported the incident, learning that no such FBI investigation was under way.

The Land Rover was reported stolen and Terry was stopped and arrested by the real police the next time he drove it. Terry had done all right as long as he ripped off the guilty. As soon as he started picking on the innocent, it was all over.[4]

CON IN THE ART WORLD

Some con artists believe that the only mark worth ripping off is a rich mark. The bigger the take from each con, the fewer cons need to be executed and the lower the chances of getting caught. Therefore, they impersonate rich people and make connections using their false identity. They get themselves invited to the right parties to get access to the rich.

One such con artist was Thomas Doyle, whose days as a phony art expert came to an end in July 2006 in New Jersey. His final scam began when Doyle got himself invited to a party at the Manhattan home of 73-year-old Norman Alexander, a well-known art collector.[5]

Alexander's home was filled with many valuable pieces of art. There were paintings by Picasso and sculptures by Rodin. The con artist told his host (and mark) how much he admired his collection. Alexander said that he was thinking about selling his art collection, along with his house. Doyle said that he might be interested in buying both the house and the collection.

Doyle scanned the painting and the sculptures. Many were too big to easily transport. Then he spotted a small bronze Rodin sculpture of a portly ballerina looking unhappily at the bottom of one foot. It was small enough to fit inside a gym bag and could be moved from one place to another without being observed.

Doyle convinced Alexander that the small statue needed to be appraised—that is, examined by an expert to determine how much it was worth. And, of course, Doyle knew just the guy to do it. He would borrow the statue, have it appraised, and then return it safely to the Alexander home.

When Doyle walked out with the statue, never to return, Alexander reported the matter to the police. Despite the thousands of dollars Alexander had invested in security systems, he had allowed a valuable piece of art to be carried right out the door.

A description of the con artist led police to arrest Doyle, but the statue was never returned. A police investigation revealed that the statue had already been sold three times and was, at that time, somewhere in Hong Kong.

Police learned that the statue was worth about $600,000, and that Doyle had sold it to an art gallery on Manhattan's Upper East Side for $225,000.[6]

The thief was charged with grand larceny and criminal possession of stolen property in July 2006. In February 2007 Doyle pleaded guilty and was sentenced to two-and-a-half to five years in prison.[7]

CHINESE CON ANTICS

One of the biggest and richest con jobs in recent years took place in China in 2007. A man by the name of Wang Zhendong impersonated a wise man of science. Under this guise, he convinced whole communities in the province of Liaoning that he had invented a system that used "mature ants" to make tea, medicine, and wine.[8]

The system was so impressive that marks thought it would change the world, and people stood in long lines for an opportunity to invest in it. An investigation by Chinese authorities revealed that Wang had no such system, and that ants, although clever, couldn't make tea, medicine, and wine. Wang was arrested. By that point, Wang had stolen 3 billion yuan, or the equivalent of $387 million.

The justice system in China is far harsher than in the United States. Wang was tried and convicted of conning thousands of people. He was sentenced to death.[9]

SCAMMING THE CHURCH

Sixty-year-old Robert Riggio, who lived in Manhattan's Lower East Side, managed to scam thousands of dollars before he was caught, and the only tool he needed was his cell phone. In 2004 Riggio went to the New York Public Library and found a directory of city rectories—the homes of New York's priests. He copied down each phone number.[10]

Over a period of months in 2006, Riggio called every priest in the city. The story he told wasn't always the same, but it was similar. He was sorry to bother them, but he had a desperate problem and he didn't know where else to turn. His mother was in some terrible jam. Sometimes she was about to be evicted from her lifelong home. Sometimes she needed money for an operation.

Author and consultant Frank Abagnale arrives for a special screening of the film *Catch Me If You Can* in December 2002. The film is based on Abagnale's life as a successful con artist. *Reuters/Corbis*

42 CONS AND FRAUDS

Riggio said he was affiliated with a parish someplace in the city, always a parish as far as possible from the priest he was calling. Could they please lend him some money to save his poor elderly mother?

Before he was caught, 60 of the priests he had called agreed. Some lent him as much as $10,000 out of their church or personal funds. The con man had made more than $200,000 by scamming the priests. Then, one of the priests, suspicious enough to check the con man's story, discovered he'd been taken and reported Riggio to the FBI. The FBI sent a female agent undercover, posing as a priest's niece.

The agent recorded Riggio making his plea for his fictional mom, and the Feds used that evidence to arrest him. The charges were wire fraud, using the telephone to commit fraud. The case awaits trial. If convicted, Riggio could be sentenced to as many as 40 years in prison.[11]

Probably the most famous impostor in recent history is Frank Abagnale Jr. Steven Spielberg made a movie about him called *Catch Me if You Can* (2002), starring Leonardo DiCaprio as Frank. The movie is based on Abagnale's best-selling autobiography.

Abagnale began impersonating others early in life. In high school he impersonated a substitute teacher and, for a time, taught French in the very school he was attending. By the time he was 19, which was in 1967, he had made more than $1 million in small cons, mostly cashing bad checks, and was impersonating a Pan Am pilot. He also successfully impersonated a doctor and a prosecuting attorney.[12]

One of Frank's most daring adventures came in 1969, when he escaped police custody while being transferred from Sweden (where he had been arrested) to the United States by climbing through a hatch beneath the airplane's rest room and hiding in the underbelly of the craft's fuselage. He then jumped from the plane as it landed at a New York airport and ran to freedom.

Though he was a great actor, he was not a master of disguise. When Abagnale's face appeared on a wanted poster, an ex-girlfriend called the cops and turned him in. After his last stint (five years) in prison, he agreed to work for the FBI (without pay) as a consultant in forged check cases. He was still only 26 years old. He went on to open a legitimate business as a consultant, helping companies recognize and prevent fraud.[13]

4

Common Scams

Imagine you operate a restaurant, perhaps a diner. A man in shabby clothes carrying a violin comes in and orders a meal. When the check comes, he reaches for his wallet and says that he must have left all of his money at home.

"I'll tell you what," the bum says. "I'll leave this violin with you. It's a priceless antique. It's my only worldly possession and playing it is how I make my living. I will leave it here, go home and get my wallet, and return to pay for the meal."

You don't like the idea but agree to it because the guy is too filthy to put to work washing dishes. Seconds after the unclean man leaves, a man in a finely tailored suit enters and sits down. He notices the violin sitting behind the counter.

"Could I see that violin for one moment," the finely dressed man says.

"Sure, a guy just left it here a few minutes ago," you say.

"Do you know what you have here? This is a one-of-a-kind Stradivarius. It is worth a *lot of money*!"

"You're kidding me," you say.

"I shouldn't say that. I should just out and out buy it from you. I would pay you, say, $400,000 cash today for it," the well-dressed man says.

You are too astonished to say anything. The well-dressed man's cell phone rings; he barks a couple of orders.

"I have to go," he says. "But I'll be back with the cash later. Don't lose that violin!"

"I won't," you reply.

The well-dressed man leaves and a few minutes later the bum returns, smiling and saying that he found his wallet. He wants to trade the price of a meal for his violin.

"Say, how would you like to sell your old fiddle?" you ask, thinking yourself clever. The bum doesn't want to. It's all he has, and he needs it to make a buck.

"I'll tell you what. I'll give you $1,000 for it. That's enough for you to buy another good violin, plus buy some new clothes," you say.

The bum reluctantly agrees. You get the cash, give it to the bum, and keep the violin. You wait for the well-dressed man to return, but he never comes back. You take the violin to be appraised and learn that it is an old, cheap fiddle not worth $50. The well-dressed man and the bum split the money and then move on to a new neighborhood or town to pull the scam again.[1]

The "fiddle game" is a classic example of the con artist using the mark's crookedness and greed against him. This chapter presents some other con games people should instantly recognize and avoid. Some of these scams are geared toward a particular type of mark. Those who fit the mold, beware.

THE BANK EXAMINER SCAM

In this con, a person posing as a bank official claims that their bank is being ripped off by an embezzler. The bank needs the mark's help to catch the criminal. In order to lure the embezzler, the official needs the mark's money, and that's where the victim gets ripped off. Before agreeing to give any bank official any money, contact the bank and make sure the official isn't an impersonator.

CLEAN CARPET CAPER

This con game is a variety of the **bait and switch** scam. Bait and switch occurs when a store advertises a sale to draw customers into the store and then—instead of giving the promised discount—charges regular or slightly higher prices. This version starts with an ad in the newspaper that offers cheap carpet cleaning for the office or home. But, once the deal is made, the cleaner says the carpet is too dirty to get the discount. An extra charge will be necessary. If this happens, report the carpet-cleaning company immediately to the Better Business Bureau.

"NONPROFIT" CONS

Many con artists pretend to represent a charity or church. Before giving money to a church or charity, ask for a verified financial statement, documentation that proves the organization is legitimate. The organization may not truly exist. Also, check out the organization to see what percent of the donated money actually goes to the charity. According to Channel 4 NBC News in Washington, D.C., "The Better Business Bureau's Philanthropic Advisory Board requires that 'a reasonable percentage,' at least fifty percent, of public contributions shall be applied to programs and activities described in solicitations."[2] You have a right to expect that your money goes where the charity says it goes.

LONELY HEARTS SCAM

Among the most vulnerable marks are the lonely. One recent scam uses the Internet to target American men. A phony dating Web site invites lonely men to meet and have online conversations with equally lonely Russian women who want to marry American men.[3]

The con artists, pretending to be lonely women, write long and loving e-mails to the marks. The crooks sometimes have 10 "conversations" going at once with different marks. The e-mails become increasingly intense and explicit. The cons write what they feel the mark wants to hear. For example, if the con senses that the mark has a fragile ego, they might write that a man is the king of the castle and that women should always obey when her man gives her an order.

The marks are told that their new friend is passionate at the thought of meeting him in person. They are told that these women are in love with them. The con men send photos to the marks, revealing the women to be young and attractive. But in order for them to meet, the "Russian women" need money for a visa and transportation.

All the woman needs is to have the money wired to her and the rest will be taken care of. She will let the mark know when she is arriving at the airport. Sometimes the con artist hits-up the mark for money a second or third time, claiming additional expenses, such as an "accident" that requires money for medical bills. She needs more to make the trip to the United States. Sometimes the mark is told that Russians are not allowed to enter the United States unless they have at least $1,500 in cash with them, because "officials" need to be "bribed"—none of which is true. Once the mark has been taken for as much money as possible, all communication stops and the lonely fellow never hears from his Internet girlfriend again.

These scams are known as Boris and Natasha schemes. The name comes from the Russian villains in the old *Bullwinkle* cartoons. The scam works because there are legitimate organizations that help Russian women get into the United States by finding them American men to marry. The typical mark gets taken for anywhere from $2,000 to $8,000.[4]

INSPECTOR SCAMS

This scam involves a person pretending to be a city or utility official who comes to the mark's home to check on the electrical wiring, the plumbing, or the heating system. The inspector will always find a problem, usually a serious problem. In an effort to win confidence, he will tell the victim that he or she can avoid a hefty fine from the city by having the problem fixed immediately. He then hands the victim a business card for his brother's plumbing business.

Before letting someone into your home, be sure to ask for identification. Before agreeing to any deals, call the city department that the "inspector" claims to represent. When checking up on a possible con, always use the phone book to get the number, not the business card you were given by the possible con artist. He may have an accomplice ready to answer the phone and back up his story.[5]

Variations on this unfortunately frequent crime include con men/burglars pretending to be from the gas company or, in one instance, sent by the church to bless the house. One keeps the homeowner, usually elderly, busy while the other searches the house for valuables.

CONTEST CON

A very common scam is the so-called contest con. The mark gets a phone call or an e-mail that says he has won a big contest.

Common Scams 47

However, before he can receive the money he must send money to the contest-holders to pay the tax on the winnings.

"Uncle Sam needs his cut up front," the con claims. Of course, a legitimate contest will simply deduct the taxes from the win-

IRISH TRAVELLERS

Some nomadic groups, usually consisting of members with the same ethnic background, use con games as part of their way of life. That's how they make a living. They scam people out of their money and then they move on. One such group, present today in the United States, is the Irish Travellers. As their name implies,

(continues)

Madelyne Toogood brought national attention to the Irish Travellers, a group that travels the country, sometimes conning people to make a living, when she was videotaped beating her daughter in a mall parking lot. *Jim Rider/AP Photo*

(continued)
they are a group of people, all of Irish ancestry, who travel from town to town together.

The Irish Travellers received unwanted publicity during late summer 2002 when a camera in an Indiana parking lot recorded a woman named Madelyne Toogood beating her small daughter inside a van. The footage was broadcast on the news worldwide. At first, it was thought to be a simple case of child abuse, and police put out an All Points Bulletin for the woman, her daughter Martha Jean, and her vehicle.

When policed traced the car to a house outside Fort Worth, Texas, they found hundreds of vehicles registered to the same address. The names on those registrations were familiar to investigators: Toogood, Burkes, Carol, Daley, Gallagher, all Irish Traveller families that cross the country scamming people out of their money.[6]

Each winter, the Toogood's clan of Irish Travellers returns to White Settlement, Texas, where they live in secrecy and isolation. Travellers arrived in the United States in the nineteenth century. They traveled the country trading mules and horses—sometimes honestly, sometimes not very honestly. They made their homes in tent camps. Some went northeast—the Northerners. Some went south toward Memphis—the Mississippi Travellers. Some went to Murphy Village, South Carolina—the Georgia Boys. Madelyne Toogood's ancestors worked their way out west. Travellers roam the country living out of trailers and hotels. Their scams range from trading in broken-down horses to home-repair scams. Traveller children grow up fast—some using fake licenses to drive when they're 12, 13, and 14. And almost all drop out of school before attending high school.[7]

Toogood's lawyer, Steven Rosen, defended her, saying he found her loyal, honest, and considerate. But, he explained, she is not educated and doesn't speak well, and because of this, she didn't come off well in the media.[8]

Don Wright, author of the book *Scam*, disagreed with the lawyer, saying, "I've never met an Irish Traveller who wasn't a con artist, and I have been associated with them for about 25 years now."[9]

nings and give the recipient a check for the remainder. Only phony contests require the so-called winner to pay before receiving the money.

TELEPHONE, REAL ESTATE, AND MEDICAL CONS

The following con is also very common. A stranger will call on the phone and explain that she needs to check something, such as unauthorized charges on the mark's credit card or insurance verification. He or she will then ask for the mark's credit card number. No one should ever give his or her credit card numbers to anyone unless ordering merchandise from a trusted source.[10]

There is a famous story about a con artist who successfully sold tourists visiting New York shares in the Brooklyn Bridge. It is unclear if that story is true, but con artists trying to sell things that either don't exist or are not what they seem are very common. Real estate is a favorite sales item. Before buying land, one should always visit the site to make sure it is real, and that it is actually for sale. Then check up on the firm making the sale and verify that it is legitimate.

The so-called Case of the Lottery Ticket Losers is another scam. Marks receive phone calls from con artists claiming that they are from a law firm representing an anonymous person who "left a winning ticket for you" in their will. In order to claim the ticket, and the multimillion-dollar prize, the mark must send money so a computer can verify his or her identity. Real life doesn't work this way. Never buy a lottery ticket from a stranger.

Another common con is the magazine subscription salesperson, who either works door to door or on the phone. The con artist in this case is usually young and has a story. She is selling subscriptions to pay her way through college, to get new uniforms for her soccer team, and so forth. The mark buys the subscriptions but the magazines never show up, and the victim never sees the con artist again.[11]

Never agree to or pay for any lab tests or medical treatments from anyone other than a trusted doctor. The lab tests will be expensive, and probably bogus. And, if someone really has health problems, bogus medical treatments can be dangerous as well as

50　CONS AND FRAUDS

In a famous scam, a con artist once allegedly sold non-existent shares of the Brooklyn Bridge to tourists visiting the Big Apple. Al Francekevich/Corbis

expensive. Con artists promising medical services usually use the U.S. mail to contact their marks, offering discounts or using frightening information to scare the marks into taking the offer. Bottom line: Consult your doctor for all tests and treatments.

Other "junk mail" letters you receive may promise cheap medical products such as diet aids, beauty products, vitamins, and cures. Sadly, seriously ill marks are often suckers for anything with the word *cure* written on it. Once the money is paid, the products either don't arrive at all or turn out to be useless or even harmful.

EMOTIONAL PLEAS AND SLEIGHT OF HAND

Remember the rule: Never trust a stranger. That's especially true when it comes to the "Help Needed" scam. A person, usually with convincing identification, says that she or a close relative is in trouble. Her car is impounded and she needs money to get it back. Her mother is sick in the hospital and she needs an operation. Any donation would help—$10 or $20 would be great. These people sometimes stand in crowded shopping areas and approach strangers, like slightly more sophisticated panhandlers. Others are bolder and go door to door, as if they are collecting money for a legitimate charity. Don't trust them, and don't give them any money.[12]

Some con men use sleight of hand to pull off their scams, working like a magician who does card tricks. One common form of this scam is the "pigeon-drop" con. It goes like this: A person says he found some money and offers to share it with the mark. In order to show his trust, he asks the victim to place the money in an envelope for safekeeping. But he asks the mark first to place some of his or her money in the envelope as a measure of good faith. Then something occurs that distracts the mark and the envelope of money is switched. The next time the victim looks, the envelope contains only paper.

Some con artists get a victim's money by getting them to unknowingly sign a contract. The most common form of this scam occurs when a door-to-door salesman is allowed inside the mark's house. The con artist will demonstrate her products and, when the victim declines to buy anything, she'll pull out a contract, saying something like, "My boss says I have to verify that I really showed you the products. Could you sign this form?" Many people sign without reading, which is unfortunate as it usually turns out to be a contract stating that the mark agrees to buy many expensive products. The products are sent to the victim, who is then charged for them. According to Patricia Holmes, "Always read every word before signing any form. Sometimes the contract continues on the back of the page. Check the back of each page before signing a contract."[13]

The "Travel Club Trick" involves a bargain airfare and/or hotel package that is offered at an exotic locale. Here's the trick: The offer is good for only one person. Most people don't want to travel alone, so the mark arranges for a second set of accommodations that he'll pay for. The price for the second traveler is double the normal rate, and thus the mark ends up buying a possibly bogus trip for two at the same price he would have been charged if the first one hadn't been "free." Check with a travel agent and read all paperwork before signing anything.

One of the oldest cons is the "Unknown Caller" scam. Two innocent-looking people, often a woman and a child, come to the door and ask to use the bathroom or for a drink. Once inside the house, one distracts the homeowner for as long as possible while the other steals everything of value that isn't nailed down. Don't let strangers into your house.[14]

GAMBLING CONS

People who enjoy playing cards for money may sometimes find themselves playing against complete strangers. There are a number of scams to avoid.

People who win money by cheating at cards are "card sharks" or "card sharps." One of the most complex card swindles is "The Big Mitt," in which a team of con men sets up an operation inside a store or other building. One of them recruits a card-playing mark from outside and invites him to play poker. The mark doesn't know that all of the other players in the game are part of a team. By stacking and hiding cards, they quickly wipe out the mark and send him on his way with his pockets pulled inside out.[15]

Another card game con is **ducats**. Here, the mark is convinced that he is on the inside of a fixed blackjack game. He is told ahead of time that all of the aces in the game have been marked on their edge so he'll be able to see them. He's to wait until he sees the penciled card and then bet all of his money for a huge score. But, when the mark is distracted, the cards are turned upside-down, and identical marks appear on different cards. The mark bets it all, loses, and the con artists take the money and get away from the mark as fast as possible.[16]

A common way for con artists to fleece their marks is to stage a fixed poker game, or, a game of "tip." In this game, the mark is usually taken for quite a bit of money and is unlikely to report the crime because he will be told up front that the game is fixed and that he is in on it. The con artist tells his mark that he knows a cruel and evil man who has just inherited millions of dollars.

Common Scams

The mark is asked, "Would you be willing to be part of a crooked poker game and take some of this man's money away?"

With dollar signs appearing in front of his eyes, the mark often agrees—eagerly. The roper says that he doesn't have to bring any of his own money. He'll supply him with money to start with.

"At first I will lose every hand to you," the roper says. They arrange for a signal so the mark will know when the roper is "bluffing."

Some gambling cons are executed using magnetized or weighted dice. George B. Diebold/Corbis

After the roper has been wiped out, he'll sit behind the millionaire and signal to the mark so the mark will know when he has a better hand than the millionaire.

They agree to meet that afternoon at a specific time and location, at which time the mark will be introduced to the millionaire and the other players of the game, all of whom are inside men working with the roper.

The mark wins quite a bit of money. Then the millionaire suggests they play one hand for a huge sum of money, more money than the mark has. The mark explains he hasn't got that kind of money on him.

"Go to an ATM and get the cash," the roper says with a wink. The mark, thinking the hand is rigged in his favor, goes to an ATM or otherwise gets the cash, and returns to the game. Naturally, the mark loses the hand and the millionaire scoops up all of the winnings.

SCAMBUSTERS

Here are some ways that law enforcement combats cons like those explained in this chapter.

- Teach potential marks about common scams so that they are less likely to fall victim to a con.
- If a con artist is working in one particular area, a law enforcement agent could go undercover and pretend to be a mark. In cases such as this, it is the con artist who is being "had."
- If a mark realizes he is being conned before the con has been completed, he could be "wired," that is, fitted with a small recording device, so that evidence can be gathered that might put the con artist in jail.
- If a lower member of a con team is arrested, he may be persuaded to, in exchange for a lesser penalty, gather evidence and testify his higher ups.

The truth is, however, that law enforcement is often not successful when it comes to arresting con artists. The criminals move from place to place and create victims who rarely report the crime.

The angry mark often confronts the roper for not signaling him properly. The roper calms the mark down by agreeing to cover the loss, and gives the mark an I.O.U. with a phony name on it. This usually relaxes the mark enough to give the roper and his inside man an opportunity to get away.[17]

Gambling cheats don't restrict their activities to cards. A common dice scam is the "Electric Bar." A magnetized plate is attached to the bottom of a thin table. A pair of dice is then rigged so that some of the dots contain metal. The metal side will always land down. The con artist can wipe out a series of marks very quickly in this fashion. Since the magnetized plate needs to be removed when the scam is through, the con artist cannot simply run away. He must get the mark to leave. A fake police raid usually works. Even a nearby guy who pulls out a police badge can get a mark to beat it, leaving his money behind.[18]

COUNTERFEIT CONS

Exchanging bundles of real money with **boodles** (stacks of fake money) is another common form of scoring illegal cash, called **laying the flue**. The con artist gets the mark to bundle up cash in some pre-arranged manner. When the mark is distracted, the con artist replaces the bundle with the boodle, and the mark leaves with a package of blank paper. In some cases, the con artist convinces the mark that his bills need to be examined for counterfeits. The money is then borrowed for examination and the boodle is returned. Another scam involves convincing the mark that the cash he just received contained a special bill that is worth millions to collectors. The man's cash will be borrowed, to be "examined" by an expert, and is then replaced.[19]

5

ID Theft

One of the leading forms of fraud today is identity (ID) theft. By pretending to be someone else, a con man purchases items for himself using the victim's credit. As with most crime, law enforcement believes the best way to crack down on ID theft is to prevent it from happening. There are some things people can do to keep their ID from being stolen. And there are things they can do, if their ID has already been stolen, to limit the damage and help catch the criminal.[1]

AN IDENTITY THEFT VICTIMS' GUIDE

Someone who suspects that his or her identity has been stolen must act quickly. The longer one waits, the more damage can be done, and the harder it will be to fix the damage.

When calling the authorities and others regarding identity theft, keep a written log of the time of each call, the phone number called, with whom you spoke, and what was said.

When possible, confirm conversations in writing. Keep copies of all written communications. Also keep track of any expenses incurred while trying to fix your problem. If the thief is caught, this might help in requesting restitution.

If credit cards, or their numbers, have been stolen, immediately contact the major credit recording companies: Experian at (888) EXPERIAN (397-3742), Equifax at (800) 525-6285, and TransUnion at (800) 680-7289. Report the theft and request a free credit report. A victim's file should be flagged with a fraud alert. Make these

(continues on page 60)

THE KIMES

Although it is true that most confidence artists are not violent, there are some who can be very dangerous. Take the case of Sante and Kenneth Kimes, a mother and son team who traveled the country, surviving by scamming and conning every mark they could find. They forged checks, stole identities to take out loans, and always stayed on the move.

However, twice during their career they felt the need to get rid of someone who was in their way. They murdered California businessman David Kazdin in 1998, and then Irene Silverman, a Manhattan millionaire, in 2000. Kazdin was killed after he discovered the duo trying to take out a $280,000 loan in his name. They

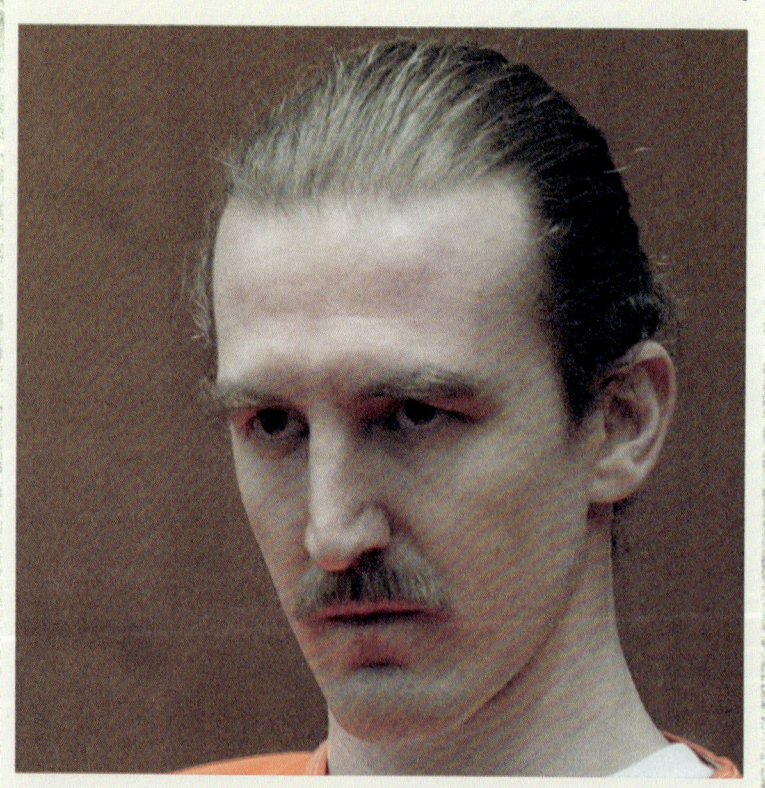

Deadly con artist Kenneth Kimes testifies in his trial for the murder of David Kazdin. Kimes testified against his mother, Sante Kimes, in order to avoid the death penalty. *Damian Dovarganes/AP Photo*

murdered Silverman after forging documents that transferred the victim's multimillion-dollar real estate business to them. In Sante Kimes' eyes, the murder was necessary to "complete the con job."

Police became suspicious of the pair soon after Silverman disappeared. A caretaker for Silverman told police that Silverman never allowed anyone to touch her keys, and that she kept $10,000 in cash in her closet. The Kimes were arrested after Kenneth was found with Silverman's keys in his pocket and Sante was found to be holding $10,000 in brand-new crisp bills.[2] Despite the fact that Silverman's body was never found, the pair was convicted of both killings and sentenced to life in prison.[3]

Sante Kimes stands trial, alongside her son and accomplice Kenneth, for the murder of David Kazdin. The mother and son's con game turned fatal when Kazdin caught the duo trying to take out a large loan in his name. *Ricardo Dearatanha/AP Photo*

CONS AND FRAUDS

(continued from page 57)

contacts both on the phone and in writing. Do not pay any bill for any goods or services not received.

The next step is to carefully read the credit report and get in touch with all creditors with whom fraud has been committed. Fill out affidavits. Blank affidavits are available at http://www.ftc.gov/bcp/edu/microsites/idtheft/.

Next, contact local police and report the crime. Request a copy of all police reports. Be prepared to show the credit report indicating the fraud, which is why it's necessary to contact the credit recording companies first.

If checks are stolen, call your bank and put stop payments on any outstanding checks, cancel all bank accounts, and open new ones. In the same vein, if an ATM card has been stolen, have it canceled immediately and get a new one. Use a new and different password. Do not use a password that can easily be guessed, such as a birthday or Social Security number. The same is true of phone service: Change phone accounts and passwords.[4]

Victims of identity theft should call a lawyer. If the thief should commit other crimes in their name, the victim will want their legal rights represented.

PRIVACY RIGHTS CONTACTS

For more information regarding individual rights to privacy and how to protect them, contact:

Privacy Rights Clearinghouse
3100 Fifth Avenue, Suite B
San Diego, CA 92103
(619) 298-3396
http://www.privacyrights.org

The Privacy Rights Clearinghouse is a nonprofit consumer organization concerned with both supplying consumers with information and helping consumers who have been wronged. It was established in 1992 and is based in San Diego, California.

If a Social Security number has been misused, a victim must contact the Social Security Administration (http://www.ssa.gov). Order a copy of your Personal Earnings and Benefits Statement and make sure it is correct.[5]

Someone who suspects an identity thief of using their postal address to commit fraud or of having submitted false change-of-address forms should immediately contact the local postal inspector. Call the United States Postal Service at (800) 275-8777 for more information about how to contact a postal inspector.

Contact the passport office whether or not you have a passport. Someone else may get a passport using a stolen identity. Log on to http://travel.state.gov/passport/passport_1738.html. Next, call the Department of Motor Vehicles to make sure no other driver's licenses have been issued in your name.[6]

If the thief is caught, be sure to write a letter to the judge of the trial itemizing the impact the theft has had on your life.[7]

THE SCOPE OF IDENTITY THEFT

There's a man from Modesto, California, who said he once bought more than $100,000 worth of merchandise using other people's identities. He said it was easy for him and others to live off of someone else's good credit.

"We'd go through the garbage of mortgage companies and department stores because they often would throw away paperwork and receipts with customers' Social Security numbers and other personal information on it," the Modesto man explained.[8]

Identity theft is nothing new. Criminals have been using false ID for decades. Shameless thieves will find records of a baby who died in infancy, but who would be around their age, and get a birth certificate. From there, it is easy.

Civilians are not the only ones at risk of ID theft. Thousands of military personnel overseas or awaiting deployment are at risk as well. In January 2003 it was reported that laptops and computer hard drives containing the names, addresses, telephone numbers, birth dates, and Social Security numbers of millions of troops had been stolen from a building in an industrial park at an undisclosed location.

The potential problems a hacker might cause became all-too-clear during January 2003, when a fast-spreading virus-like infection struck the Internet and slowed Web traffic and e-mail all around the world. According to the FBI, the virus resembled blueprints for a computer code that had been published several weeks before on a Chinese computer-hacking Web site. According to Howard Schmidt, a presidential cybersecurity adviser, disruption to the U.S. government was "minimal." The incident did expose the Internet's vulnerability, however, as well as the inadequacy of the security measures adopted for computer networks.[9] The worry remains that a smart hacker might be able to commit crimes that could affect national security, such as stealing the identitites of government or military personnel.

E-Cons:
Scamming on the Grifter Superhighway

In a world of Google, YouTube, Amazon.com, and eBay, it should surprise no one that con artists have kept up with the times.

THE ADVANCE-FEE CON

In 2002 the British Broadcasting Company (BBC) reported on a con scheme that was enjoying great success in West Africa. Criminals there used a fake version of a British bank's online service to separate their marks from their cash. The United Kingdom's National Criminal Intelligence Service (NCIS) said at least two Canadians had lost more than $100,000 after being taken in by the fake Web site. The Web site offered interested parties a tempting portion of the huge sums of money they needed to move out of various African nations and asked the marks to pay the necessary fees to do so.

Apparently there is something uniquely seductive about Internet scams. According to NCIS officials, victims who otherwise might have seen through the scam were taken in because it was on the Web.

Also, according to the BBC, con artists had used an unclaimed Web domain of a British bank to fleece victims.

"I have seen the microsite myself and it's very sophisticated," said the NCIS spokesman. "It's very convincing, especially to people not very experienced online."[1]

Defendant Obum Osakwe arrives at court in Nigeria in February 2004. He and four others stood trial for defrauding a Brazilian bank of $242 million in one of the biggest "419" scams brought to trial in Nigeria. *George Esiri/Reuters/Corbis*

Once the con was discovered, it was quickly shut down. However, the people behind it were not caught, and no doubt moved on to create their next confidence game. The bank involved immediately bought the domain used in the con as well as many other variations of its name to limit the chance it could happen again.

The BBC reported, "Like any con, there is no money to be moved at all and instead anyone taking the bait is asked to pay increasingly large sums to supposedly bribe uncooperative officials and to smooth the passage of the cash. Although this con has been practiced for years, people still fall victim to it." The West African scam is known as an "advance fee" or "419" con. Marks receive unsolicited e-mails. (A few years ago, the initial contact

THE SPANISH PRISONER

As evidence that con games have been around a long time and have not changed much, the "advance-fee" con can be traced back to the 1500s, when it was known as "the Spanish prisoner."[2]

In that version of the con, the con artist told the mark that he had been exchanging letters with a rich man who had been imprisoned in Spain by King Philip II. In this con, it doesn't really matter what country or what ruler. The con artist updates and adjusts as he goes to suit the times and the prejudices of the mark. The rich man, the mark is told, has been arrested and incarcerated under a false name. The prisoner cannot reveal his true identity or else there would be dire consequences, so he is relying on the con artist to raise the funds necessary to bribe for his release. If the mark were to contribute money to this cause, everyone would make money in fistfuls after the prisoner was released and used his riches to reward those who had helped him purchase his freedom. Usually, more than one payment is necessary: A difficulty inevitably arises and more money is needed. When the mark has been fleeced to the max, the con artist disappears.[3]

The "Spanish prisoner" con, or variations thereof, have been used as plot elements in two movies directed by David Mamet, *The Spanish Prisoner* (1997) and *House of Games* (1987).[4]

would have come by fax.) The e-mail offers a share of any cash successfully moved out of Africa. The *419* refers to the part of the Nigerian penal code dealing with such crimes.[5]

The NCIS has managed to hinder Internet scams. A spokesman for the NCIS talked about an earlier, more successful investigation into a confidence game involving the Internet and banking. He said:

> To many people nowadays the cutting edge of banking technology is Web technology. One of the first groups of con men to use this method set up a fake Web site that supposedly gave victims access to accounts held at the South African Reserve Bank, the country's national bank. Typically, victims are given a login name and password and are encouraged to visit the site so they can see that the cash they are getting a share of has been deposited in their name. But before they can get their hands on the cash, the victims are typically asked to hand over more of their own money to help the transfer go ahead. Once the South African police discovered the ruse they declared it a national priority crime and soon arrested the eighteen people behind it.[6]

PHISHING AND SPAM

Anyone with access to e-mail and the Internet could be the victim of phishing, a relatively new form of con game, or the so-called spam scam. Phishing begins with an unwanted e-mail, the type of e-mail known as spam. An e-mail or pop-up message is sent from a business, organization, or government agency asking the recipient to update or validate information about their account. The message asks for an immediate response.

Recipients should not open any attachment, reply, or click on links within the message, as this may release a computer virus or allow a con artist to collect personal data, such as passwords. Be sure to keep anti-virus computer software up to date. Complaints may be filed at http://www.ftc.gov/bcp/edu/microsites/idtheft/ at the Federal Trade Commission's identity theft Web site or call toll free (877) FTC-HELP (382-4357).[7]

It might seem that con artists who make a living by phishing would find their strongest opposition from law enforcement,

E-Cons 67

A woman checks her e-mail. Because of the rise of phishing and spam scams, it is important to be especially cautious when dealing with mail from an unknown sender. Helen King/Corbis

but that is not the case. As it turns out, phishing's number-one enemy has been fellow computer pranksters who release hard-drive-destroying viruses on the Internet. Home computer owners quickly learned that, if they didn't want to allow a virus or a worm into their machine, they should not open any attachments to any e-mails unless they knew and trusted the source.

According to the Gannett newspaper *USA Today*, "A batch of e-mails recently making the rounds were crafted to appear as if they came from PayPal, eBay's online payment service. Like traditional phony 'phishing' e-mails, these said there was some problem with the recipients' accounts. Phishing e-mails generally instruct recipients to click a link in the e-mail to confirm their personal information; the link actually connects to a bogus site where the data are stolen. But with Internet users wiser about phishing, the new fake PayPal e-mail included no such link. Instead it told users to call a number, where an automated answering service asked for account information."[8]

All too often, the scam worked. And, other than educating the public to be on the lookout for such scams, there was nothing law enforcement could do about it. Security experts tracked the scam, but because of present technology, it is impossible to locate and arrest such sophisticated con artists.[9]

"It is becoming more difficult to distinguish phishing attempts from actual attempts to contact customers," said Ron O'Brien, a security analyst with Sophos PLC.

The frauds mimic the legitimate ways people interact with financial institutions. Some phishing-like scams don't begin with an e-mail. Some begin with phone calls in which the caller already knows the recipient's credit card number—increasing the perception of legitimacy—and asks just for the valuable three-digit security code on the back of the card. This is vishing, short for *voice phishing*. *USA Today* reported that vishing appears to be flourishing with the help of Voice over Internet Protocol, or VoIP, the technology that enables cheap and anonymous Internet telephone calls, as well as the ease with which caller ID boxes can be tricked into displaying erroneous information.[10]

"If you get a telephone call where someone is asking you to provide or confirm any of your personal information, immediately hang up and call your financial institution with the number on the back of the card," said Paul Henry, a vice president with Secure Computing Corp. "If it was a real issue, they can address the issue."[11]

During the autumn of 2006, the following example of a phishing e-mail was sent to millions of people. (Text reprinted verbatim, complete with grammatical errors.):

Greetings, I apologized using this medium to reach you for a transaction/business of this magnitude, but this is due to

Confidentiality and prompt access reposed on this medium. In unfolding this proposal, I want to count on you, as a respected and honest person to handle this project/transaction with sincerity, trust and confidentiality. Let me use this opportunity to introduce myself briefly to you. I am Charles Martin, Minister of Foreign Affairs Ministry, Spain. My office monitors and controls the affairs of all banks and financial institutions in my country concerned with foreign contract payments. I am the final signatory to any transfer or remittance of funds moving within banks both on the local and international levels in line to foreign contracts settlement. I have before me, list of funds which could not be transferred to some nominated accounts as these accounts have been identified either as ghost accounts, unclaimed deposits or over-invoiced sum etc. Now listen carefully please. I write to present you to the federal government that you are among the people expecting the funds to be transferred into their accounts. On this note, I wish to have a deal with you as regards to the unpaid certified contract funds. I have every file before me and the data's will be changed into your name to enable you receive the fund into your nominated account as the contractor/beneficiary of the fund amount (20 Million Euros.) It is my duty to recommend the transfer of these surplus funds to the federal government treasury and reserve accounts as unclaimed deposits. I have the opportunity to write you based on the instructions I received 2 days ago from the Senate Committee on Contract Payments to Foreign Debts to submit the list of payment reports / expenditures and audited reports of revenues. Among several others, I have decided to remit this sum following my idea that we have a deal/agreement and I am going to do this legally.

My conditions as follows: 1. You will give me and my colleagues 65% at of the total sum as soon as you confirm the total fund in your designated account. 30% will be for you for your effort while 5% should be set aside for any miscellaneous expenses. 2. This transaction must be kept highly secretive as I am still in service to avoid public notice and all correspondence will be strictly by email for security purposes. We will talk on phone partially if any warrant for that. 3. There should be no third parties as most problems associated with your fund release are caused by your agents or representative. If you agree with my conditions, I will intimate you with the procedures to enable me fix your name on the payment schedule instantly to meet the three days mandate. I hope you don't reject this offer as this great opportunity comes but once in one's entire life. Conclusively, I look forward to hearing from you soonest. Regards, Charles Martin.[12]

Tempted? Don't do it! There is no telling how many people fell for this scam, and the chances that law enforcement will ever catch the con artist responsible are slim. Until scam-chasing technology catches up with the criminals' ability to remain anonymous, educating potential marks is the best way to minimize the damage.

Here's another scam to avoid, although it's hard: The victim gets an e-mail from an official-sounding address. It says that their records show that his credit card is being used in an unusual way, and they wanted to warn him about it. Their records indicate that he has been charged $5,000 for nineteenth-century Spanish first-edition books, and if he did not make this purchase, he should call a given phone number to confirm.

Naturally, the mark's first thought is, "I've never bought a nineteenth-century Spanish book in my life, not even second editions!" So he calls the number to confirm and gives the operator his name, credit card number, and expiration date.

He has just had his identity stolen.

The operator is not with a credit card company. He is a con artist.[13]

Once a mark, always a mark, the belief seems to be. Some Internet scams are designed to fleece those who have just been the victim of an Internet scam. A spam e-mail asks, "Been Ripped Off? We'll get your money back!" They call themselves "recovery rooms" and (for a fee) promise that they will get a victim's money back. There may be a number to call. If the mark calls, someone claiming to be a lawyer or a recovery expert will talk him into paying a fee up front for which, in return, he will get absolutely nothing. Any real lawyer seeking to help someone recover lost funds would not demand money up front but would take a percentage of the recovered money or bill for services after they have been provided.

Catching scamsters who work this way is very difficult because the Internet is anonymous. It can be impossible to locate the source of an e-mail, especially if it has been repeatedly forwarded through a spam system.[14]

The scams work the same way, no matter what. The mark ends up without his money and, if the service or merchandise ordered actually exists, it isn't anything like it was described.

WEB SITE IMPOSTORS

Some Internet con artists use so-called spoof sites. A spoof site is a spam e-mail that has been designed to mimic the look of a famous Web site, such as Amazon.com or eBay. The e-mail, a typical phishing letter, will say that there is a problem with the recipient's account. Those who have no account with that site will ignore the spam, but a percentage of those that do will take it seriously. Anyone who clicks on the link appears to be taken to the familiar site. In reality, it is a counterfeit. The con artists want the victim to confirm information for them, and there are blanks for a name, credit card number, etc. The mark fills in the blanks, clicks the mouse, and gets ripped off. Within minutes the credit card will be charged with expensive, luxury items, used before the mark can act to have the card canceled.[15]

At least some of the difficulties law enforcement has in combating Internet fraud are the same as they experience in fighting con games in general. It is hard to get victims to come forward. Before a crime can be investigated, law enforcement needs to know that the crime occurred. Sometimes finding out that a swindle happened can be the hardest step in bringing a con artist to justice. On the other hand, undercover agents posing as marks can do so without leaving their desk.

Law enforcement has not been completely ineffective in investigating and arresting Internet con artists. Through 2006, FBI operations have resulted in 13 indictments and 44 convictions.[16]

Local police in England recently busted an Internet scam, this one also involving eBay. Criminals were conning sellers on the Web site into believing that items purchased had already been paid for. They did this by creating real-looking Paypal letters informing the sellers that the appropriate amount of money had been transferred into their account. The sellers didn't realize that no such payments had been made until after the items had been mailed. Because the scam involved actual merchandise rather than just identities, a real address was needed to receive the stolen items, which helped lead to the arrest of Temitope Otukoya and Olamrewaju Otukoya in October 2007.[17]

World Without Shame

The world of con games lacks a conscience. FBI profilers might call con artists sociopathic. They feel no remorse, no guilt. And so the cons continue, defying both law and human decency.

ELUDING JUSTICE

Con men know that, if they keep committing the same crime over and over again in the same region of the world, sooner or later they are going to get caught. But before they can be put in prison, they must be arrested, tried, convicted, and sentenced.

To prevent doing time behind bars, con artists have been known to use their social skills to determine who in the law enforcement community is corrupt and then bribe those people. In many cases, they bribe, or **fit the mitt**, of local officials before there is even an arrest.

If the correct people have had their palms greased, then the chances are slim that the con artist will ever do time in prison. This is the **fix**. Con artists consider it to be like insurance. They don't have to worry about being arrested because they have purchased, to put it in Monopoly terms, a "Get Out of Jail Free" card.

In some cases, bribed community officials are not paid a single amount but rather receive a percentage of each "touch," or successful con. Because of this, it is in the official's best financial interests to keep the con artist free to conduct his illegal activities.

It is common for con artists to bribe local officials or members of organized crime to avoid punishment for their crimes. Push Pictures/ Corbis

In larger cities, the con man does not fix his operation directly through the public official but rather through a member of organized crime. A fee is paid to the mobster, and the mobster informs officials who are already on board that there is a con artist at work and he is to be left alone.

The "fixer," the mob go-between, may receive as much as 17 percent of every touch. If a con artist scams $100,000 from a mark, as much as $17,000 of that will go to the fixer. As long as the con artist has money and the corrupt officials he is bribing remain in their positions, the con artist does not have to worry.[1]

MANIPULATING EMOTIONS

Some con artists are worse than shameless. They are heartless. They often get away with their cons because nice people cannot fathom anyone behaving in such an evil manner without being crippled by shame.

Take for example a parent who shaves his child's head to make him or her look ill, and then collects money for that child's "cancer treatments." Victims cannot believe that anyone would be so lacking in dignity that they would attempt such a scheme. In that shameless category falls one Scott Fredericks, who, for years, faked paralysis so he could collect $1,350 per day in taxpayer assistance.[2]

The beginning of the end for Fredericks came one day in 2006, when he called a reporter for the *New York Daily News* and pretended to be a New York cop. Speaking in a thick Brooklyn accent, the man said, "I'm an NYPD cop. I'm in Queens Hospital with a

CASE OF THE PERISHED PARTNER

Another example of con artists living in a shame-free world became public in 2003, when a con artist named Patric Henn was arrested in Florida for fraud. He claimed that he was a gay man whose partner had been killed in the 9/11 attacks. He was so persistent in his claim that he managed to bilk $68,000 out of the American Red Cross. Police became suspicious of his claim when they learned that he was already wanted in Texas. A check revealed that the partner the man claimed to have lost never existed. Henn pleaded guilty to fraud charges in 2005, and was sentenced to two-and-a-half years in prison.[3]

Henn was not alone. A man named Carlton McNish told authorities his wife had died on 9/11 in the World Trade Center. He received more than $100,000 from charities such as the Red Cross before it was revealed that he had no wife. Authorities first became suspicious when McNish had trouble spelling his wife's name.[4]

According to Manhattan District Attorney Robert M. Morgenthau, by 2003, almost 250 people were arrested and charged with crimes related to World Trade Center fraud.[5]

76 CONS AND FRAUDS

perp on another case. There is a guy here who's got no family, no friends, he's paralyzed from the waist down and they are abusing the hell out of him."

The reporter asked why he didn't take care of the situation himself, since he was supposedly a cop. The man said, "I could jeopardize the badge. This is not my turf. I just can't. It's complicated."

Donald Adair defrauded the American Red Cross and the Federal Emergency Management Agency of thousands of dollars meant for victims of Hurricane Katrina. *Mel Evans/AP Photo*

The reporter researched the case and quickly determined that the "cop" who had called her and the paralysis victim were the same man. The 45-year-old Fredericks had a long list of bizarre crimes on his rap sheet, which covered more than 20 years. He frequently posed as a cop. He was once arrested for embezzling $114,000 in Medicaid funds by posing as his own home health aide.

"I run into a lot of strange people in my work," said Fredericks's court-appointed guardian. "This guy was probably the strangest and the most intelligent. He is like an idiot savant. He could charm the pants off of people." When the reporter visited the man in the hospital, she found that he was pretending to be an invalid so that his every want and need could be tended to, at the taxpayer's expense. He would be flirting with a nurse one minute and complaining that the hospital staff was beating him up the next.

One attorney commented, "Now he says he can't move his arms and hands. Nurses have to feed him, hold the phone up to his ear. In fact, at some point I had to feed him! I said to myself, 'What am I doing?'"

Research into Fredericks's background revealed he was a man who had a photographic memory, who could play the violin, and spoke many languages. He attended Ohio State University. His first arrest during the 1980s was for stealing a car. When police searched his home, they found a dark blue police uniform, various police identification cards, and a .357 magnum revolver. His car was equipped with a flashing light and siren. He was found guilty and given probation. In 2004 he was arrested for impersonating a police commissioner and driving with forged license plates and a forged ID. It was apparently at that point that he began faking paralysis so that he could stay in a hospital bed rather than a prison cell. He had moved from hospital to hospital as he wore out his welcome again and again.

"Our hospital did everything it could to get him placed in an alternative setting," said a spokesman at Bronx-Lebanon in New York, one of several hospitals where Fredericks spent time. "We are a busy hospital, at capacity level, and there are 25 sick people every day in our emergency room who need that bed."

But Fredericks's days of freedom may be coming to an end. According to the New Year's Eve 2006 edition of the *New York Daily News*, "After years of flimflamming, Scott Fredericks may have finally met his match in U.S. District Court Judge Paul Crotty. When Scott Fredericks missed several court appearances, the judge had him arrested in his hospital bed and ordered him to undergo physical and neurological exams he had resisted for years—or go straight to jail." As this is written, he is awaiting trial on health care fraud charges.[6]

Public Education and Protection Against Cons

One of the most popular methods of combating confidence games is to educate the public about them. The more people know about a swindle, the less likely they are to be taken.

INTERNATIONAL EFFORTS

During the summer of 2006 an international task force against cross-border fraud was set up. It consisted of the FBI and the Royal Canadian Mounted Police (RCMP).

The task force teaches ordinary people how to avoid getting ripped off. Students are taught to guard against scams pulled by telemarketers, spam e-mailers, and misleading advertisers (bait and switch).[1]

The assistant director of the Los Angeles Office of the FBI said the U.S./Canadian border should not be considered an "invisible shield by which fraud is committed, since both countries have committed to protecting their citizens."[2]

Here, according to the FBI/RCMP task force, are the seven things consumers should be aware of to avoid becoming a victim:

1. If it sounds too good to be true, it probably is.
2. Fraudulent telemarketers may misrepresent themselves as government officials, police, attorneys, etc. Never believe a person is who they say they are over the phone.

3. Actual winners of a prize or lottery never have to pay a fee up front in order to collect their cash.
4. If someone on the phone attempts to get you to pay a fee to collect a prize or cash winnings, hang up immediately.
5. Never provide personal information, such as Social Security numbers, credit card numbers, or bank account information over the phone or Internet.
6. Do not attempt to cash or deposit checks sent by telemarketers in order to pay fees and taxes on a forthcoming prize of cash winnings. The checks might appear legitimate, but they are not.
7. Be aware that fraudulent telemarketers will often express urgency. The money to pay the fee in order to collect your prize must be handed over immediately, or the prize will go to someone else. Actual lotteries and contests do not work this way.[3]

A SUCCESS STORY

Here's an example of a scam that was so well thought out, there seemed to be no hope of stopping it. Only inter-agency cooperation and a flexible body of lawmakers could put an end to it.

The setup for the con game was a small petting zoo on the road leaving Yellowstone National Park in Montana. A small fee was charged, and families with children used the outhouses and the kids were allowed to pet the farm animals for a few minutes.

In cases in which the travelers were more than 1,000 miles away from home (which could be determined by looking at their license plates), with multiple females and *one* male, the male was separated from the others and became the mark.

While the others looked at the animals, he was distracted and led into a small shack with a gambling parlor inside. The game was

HOW TO REPORT ADVANCE FEE SCAMS

Report cross-border or advance-fee scams to the FBI's Internet Crime Complaint Center: http://www.ic3.gov. To report crimes committed over the phone, call PhoneBusters at (888) 495-8501. To report deceptive advertising practices, call the Federal Trade Commission at (877) 382-4357.[4]

that every bet had to be double the previous bet. It was a game he couldn't lose. Even if his number didn't come up the first few times, he had to win that money back because, when he did win, he would have that much more money to bet. The trouble was that the game was rigged and the mark's number never came up. He continued to double his bets until his wallet was empty, at which time he was told that he had to leave.

The scam worked because never once did the mark scream bloody murder that he had been robbed while still at the petting zoo. In every case for almost a decade, the people got back in their car and drove away without a word. The man, in a car full of women, was too ashamed to admit right away that he had lost the vacation money. He was often many miles away before he admitted that it had happened. Even then, very few thought they could do anything about it.

The man simply thought he had been a fool and lost the money. Those who did contact police were told that only the local police near the petting zoo could do anything about it. Giving up, the tourists had money wired to them so they could afford to get home.

On rare occasions, people did return to the county of the petting zoo to swear out a complaint, but in no case were the victims willing to stay in town long enough to be a witness in a criminal prosecution or return to the town at a future date so they could testify at a trial.

And, even if there was a witness to the scam who was willing to testify against the petting zoo, what exactly would he testify to? All he knows is that he gambled and lost. He may know that it was a rip-off, but he doesn't have a clue as to how it was done. His statement that he had been robbed might not be enough to convince a jury.

But the operation was successfully shut down following a successful prosecution, a case which led to a change in Montana law that made it much easier from then on to bring con artists to justice.[5]

In this case, the crime was reported in one state to a police department, and investigated by a police department in another state. Initially, no prosecution could take place because the confidence game law in Montana was too vague. The state had to prove that the gambling included a "device" that was "rigged." The state legislature shored up the law, however, redefining a confidence game as one in which the mark never won. In this manner the state no longer had to prove that sleight of hand had occurred, only that the results never favored the mark.

Once the law was changed, undercover agents—always men with out-of-state license plates traveling with women—were able to gather evidence that all gamblers who played the game lost their money—quickly and in the same way.

These criminals were busted, but that doesn't mean that there aren't hundreds and maybe thousands of crooked, illegal gambling operations underway all over the United States. The best way to stop these cons is to make tourists smarter. Gambling is never a good idea, but it is an especially bad idea if you are gambling in an unregulated situation. In other words, people who must gamble should stick to a legal race track, a state-regulated off-track betting parlor, or a legal casino. At least there they have a (small) chance of winning.

MAGIC FINGERS

Since the law isn't designed to expose magic tricks, criminal proceedings against con artists are extremely rare. Much of what is known about the confidence game comes from con artists discussing their skills as well as from victims describing how they were ripped off.

In Australia a former con man transformed his criminal career into a show business act. He is Nicholas J. Johnson, the Honest Con Man, and he bills himself as "a con man, a pickpocket, a magician, a comedian, a mind reader, and a sideshow performer all rolled into one!"

He started out setting up a "bunco booth" at carnivals and ended up becoming a TV star, called by one commentator, "Australia's number-one con man."

Among Johnson's claims, which the public is not fully expected to believe but might nonetheless be true, are that he once picked an FBI agent's pocket, cheated a Royal Canadian Mounted Police officer at cards, and three years in a row predicted the first three finishers, in order, in Australia's number-one annual horse race.

During TV appearances, Johnson warns viewers of scams to avoid, and performs sleight-of-hand tricks that—in a show-biz

Public Education and Protection Against Cons

fashion—blur the line between crime and magic. At parties and functions, he will, for a fee, allow guests to participate in a fixed card game. Nobody really loses their money, though. It's just for fun. Johnson's act helps inform the public about common cons, how they work, and how to avoid them.[6]

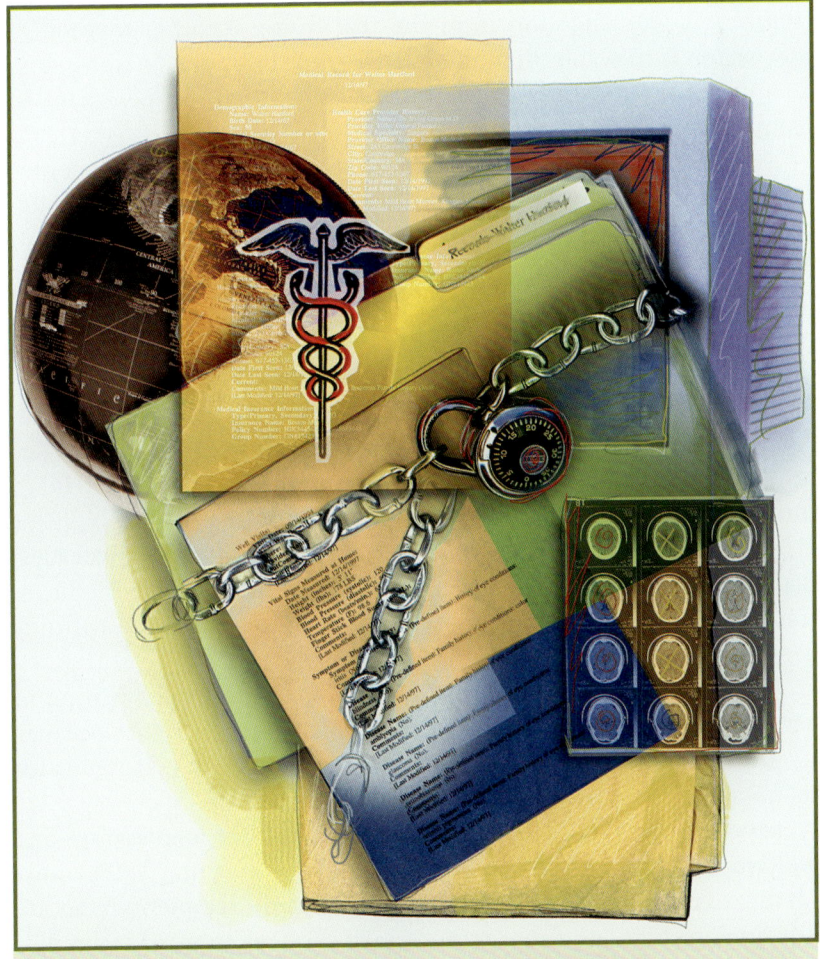

To make sure that a person receiving medical treatment is the same person collecting insurance benefits, it is especially important to keep medical records and insurance information secure. *Images.com/Corbis*

PROTECTING MEDICARE RECIPIENTS

One of the most common forms of fraud is using assumed identities and fake identification to collect Medicare benefits illegally. One way to hinder these types of crimes is to educate health care employees to better weed out and report those who are trying to illegally receive Medicare payments. Those who process patients in doctor's offices and hospitals should be taught to better distinguish counterfeit identification from the real thing. Another method of prevention is to teach them the telltale signs of impersonators, such as unusual nervousness and reluctance to show multiple forms of identification.

A more aggressive strategy to combat Medicare fraud comes from Brooklyn, New York, District Attorney Joe Hynes. He suggested to New York Attorney General Andrew Cuomo that all Medicare recipients should be fingerprinted, thus seemingly assuring that the patient who is receiving the treatment is the same person who qualifies for the benefits.

Hynes told the *New York Post*, "I think if someone is getting public money, it's perfectly appropriate to have them fingerprinted. I have in my pocket a shield and an ID, and I have to be fingerprinted for that. I'm getting public money. I don't think it is an intrusion at all."

Hynes had been on the Medicare fraud beat for three decades. Back in the 1980s he had been New York State's first Medicare fraud investigator. Cuomo appointed Hynes the head of the attorney general's Medicaid Fraud Control Unit.

Civil rights advocates had protested that the fingerprinting of Medicare applicants is a violation of a person's civil rights because it "stigmatizes applicants and discourages them from getting health insurance."

Hynes pointed out that New York recipients of food stamps and welfare benefits are all fingerprinted, and that since 1997, most Medicare recipients are fingerprinted. The only recipients who are not fingerprinted are those who receive services in nursing homes. Fingerprinting those who receive public funds has been effective in the past in the war on fraud. When New York City Mayor Rudy Giuliani implemented a fingerprinting program for welfare recipients, the number of people receiving funds plummeted, as those who were ineligible no longer received money. The same savings in tax money could be expected if all Medicare recipients were fingerprinted, Hynes argued.[7]

Again and again, con artists rely on the gullibility of the public to execute their crimes. Plus, they rely on the embarrassment of being victimized and the seeming helplessness of the individual to keep con artist crimes from being reported. By making individuals less gullible, more willing to admit that they've been had, and knowledgeable as to what to do once they've been victimized, law enforcement can cut down on confidence-game crime simply by making marks harder to find.

The systematic fingerprinting of Medicare recipients is one proposed method for combating fraud. *Ralf Tooten/Corbis*

Media Investigations:
60 Minutes

Fighting confidence games and fraud was once an activity exclusively undertaken by law enforcement. Over the past several decades, though, investigative journalism has become an important part of combating cons. Newspaper and television reporters have begun to play a big role in exposing con artists and other fraudulent activities. Newspapers such as the *New York Times* and the *Washington Post*, as well as TV shows like *60 Minutes* and *20/20* have exposed such rackets. With the journalists themselves conducting and documenting the investigation, law enforcement's job is made easy. Arrests, prosecutions, and convictions often follow the breaking story.

60 MINUTES

The popular CBS show *60 Minutes* has exposed many con artists during the decades it has been on the air. It exposed Bill Whitlow, whose business was turning back the odometers on cars to increase their resale value. Reporter Steve Kroft went undercover with a hidden camera and microphone and learned about the business by pretending to be an interested investor. Whitlow was taped admitting that he made tons of dough pulling the same scam over and over again, and that he hadn't paid any income tax for 14 years. The tapes

PYRAMID SCHEME

A pyramid scheme involves a con artist who convinces investors to give money to those above him in the pyramid (earlier investors), with the expectation that they will receive money from those below him in the pyramid. Since pyramids are thick at the bottom and narrow at the top, the mark assumes that he will receive more money than he pays out. Each investor is urged to go out and recruit new members. Usually, the con line goes something like this: If everyone can recruit five investors, and those investors recruit five investors, we'll all be millionaires! Of course, it doesn't work. Only those at the very top of the pyramid (the con artists themselves) make any money. The rest are marks. Pyramids are illegal in all 50 states and by the laws of most nations.

were not only broadcast on the show, but they were turned over to police as well. Whitlow ended up serving seven years in prison.[1]

In 1985 reporter Diane Sawyer exposed a scam in which, for $16,500 a pop, a counterfeiter was selling medical degrees. These degrees, once purchased, allowed con artists to set up "doctor's" offices that appeared real. The con artists could use these spaces to practice medicine without a license or as the big store to run other con games. Sawyer encountered one man who had been working as a doctor, both in an office and in a hospital, for 10 years without being an actual physician.[2]

One particularly damaging scam exposed by the show was a pyramid scheme that grew so large that it affected, and worsened, the economy of an entire nation. In 1996 and 1997 much of the population of Albania was fleeced. The nation had not long before been under Communist rule. Concepts such as personal investing were new to the Albanian people. When brand new investment firms popped up in the country, some were bogus. It is estimated that, at one point, two-thirds of the working adults in Albania had at least some of their money tied up in the illegal pyramid scheme. A percentage of the country's worth had been sucked away by a con artist before people began realizing that they were not going to get their money back. When the scam was revealed, there were

Media Investigations

riots in which 2,000 people were killed and the government was overthrown.[3]

The program also exposed con artists who dealt in literary scams—books and authors that weren't what they claimed to be. In 1983 a con artist sold the diaries of Adolf Hitler, the leader of Nazi Germany before and during World War II. When the public first learned of them, a man with the bogus name Dr. Fischer had already sold the diaries for 10 million marks to a German magazine called *Stern*.

Police use a water cannon to try to disperse protesters in Lushnja, Albania, in January 1997. The protesters blamed the government for the money they lost in pyramid schemes that collapsed. *Hektor Pustina/AP Photo*

90 CONS AND FRAUDS

Magazines and newspapers from other countries were lined up to publish the diaries at the same time. Two million copies of the diaries were printed before German forgery experts asked to look at the documents.

It was quickly determined that the diaries were fake—and not even very good fakes. The police investigated and learned that "Dr. Fischer" was actually Konrad Kujau, a forger and Hitler expert. He was arrested and spent three years in prison.[4]

Konrad Kujau stands in his art gallery displaying only copies and fakes in March 1989. Kujau served a three-year jail sentence after he was unmasked for forging 62 volumes of Adolf Hitler's so-called diary in 1983. *Regis Bossu/Sygma/Corbis*

PONZI SCHEME

Named after Charles Ponzi, who ran the scam in 1919, a Ponzi scheme is a con in which early investors in a fake enterprise are paid entirely with money received from more recent investors. This encourages early investors to invest even more money. When the con artists pockets are full of cash, the scheme—whatever it is—falls through. The investors are robbed of their money and the con artist has moved on. Although similar in nature to a pyramid scheme, the perpetrator of a Ponzi scheme interacts directly with his marks. The con artist behind a pyramid scheme encourages the marks to recruit new victims independently.

Con artist Charles Ponzi, after whom the Ponzi scheme is named. *Bettmann/Corbis*

92 CONS AND FRAUDS

American author and fraudster Clifford Irving pictured during a visit to London in 1977. *Hulton-Deutsch Collection/Corbis*

Another famous scam, this one by a writer, came during the 1970s, when Clifford Irving claimed to have the autobiography of billionaire Howard Hughes. Irving probably figured that there would be no way to prove that the book was a fake since Hughes was a recluse and had not been seen or heard from in many years. Irving had been an actual published author for years. Even though Howard Hughes hadn't written this book, Irving (as a writer) wanted everything to be as correct as possible. He did his research.

Irving's plans to publish the book went wrong when Hughes himself (or a clever impostor pretending to be Hughes) called the media on January 7, 1972, and said he'd never heard of Irving. The authorities stepped in and arrested Irving for fraud.

Three weeks later Irving confessed that the book was a fake. He'd never met Hughes. He had to pay back the $750,000 he had received from a publisher and serve 14 months in prison.

When interviewed years later by *60 Minutes*, Irving explained that believing the lie was the key to being a successful con artist. Irving said, "I convinced myself that I knew Howard Hughes intimately. You wondered how I could lie so well to you. I believed everything I was telling you. I believed we met. I believed I knew his life better than any 'real' biographer, because I had imagined it."[5]

Irving's story was turned into a major motion picture called *Hoax* (2006), starring Richard Gere as the con man. Irving's attempted scam was very gutsy. Most con men do not attempt to scam the entire world or to do it while the focal point of a frenzied media.

The most successful con man *60 Minutes* ever exposed was Dr. John Ackah Blay-Miezah, who claimed to be the richest man in the world. He claimed to be in sole possession of something called the Oman-Ghana fund and that he needed other people's money in order to free up the funds. He promised that he would eventually pay out $10 for every $1 he received. Without giving much more detail than that, people were waiting in line to invest in the fund.

In January 1989, *60 Minutes*, with Ed Bradley reporting, ran a piece on the man, saying that, despite the fact that he had accumulated close to $1 billion using his story, he had yet to pay out a dime. When Bradley interviewed the man in person, "[Blay-Miezah] was living in luxury in London, thanks to the gullibility and greed of his American investors whom he'd bilked." Blay-Miezah died sometime in the late 1990s, before authorities had an opportunity to get back any of the money he'd stolen.[6]

This is a sampling of the most common cons and frauds. The world contains many con artists who are on the constant lookout for marks. There are only two rules to remember to avoid becoming a mark: Never trust a stranger, and if it sounds too good to be true, it probably is.

Chronology

1900s   Kayfabe, the language of con artists and grifters, originates.

1904   James Whitaker Wright, one of the first con men to work on a grand scale, is convicted of selling fake silver mines.

1939   *You Can't Cheat an Honest Man,* a comedy classic about a con artist, starring and written by W. C. Fields, is released.

1940s   Police form first bunco squads.

1962   Meredith Wilson's award-winning Broadway musical *The Music Man* becomes a movie. The story revolves around a con artist who convinces people that juvenile delinquency will ruin their town unless he, a well-known music teacher and bandleader, transforms the young people into a marching band with "76 trombones." The people pay up front for the instruments and the uniforms, all of which are never intended to arrive. The con artist has a hard time sneaking out of town, though, because he has fallen in love—with a pretty girl and with the town.[1]

1970   Congress passes the RICO laws, making it easier to prosecute groups of con artists working together. The new laws allow law enforcement to arrest criminals who are part of a racket, or a conspiracy to commit a crime. Racketeering laws become a new weapon against confidence games, allowing people who lose money because of a con game to sue the con artist to get their money back in triplicate.

1972   With an autobiography of Howard Hughes about to go to press, the reclusive billionaire himself calls seven journalists and states he has never heard of Clifford Irving, the author who had the manuscript. Irving confesses to making the whole thing up and spends 14 months in prison.

1978 William H. Webster takes over as FBI director. To combat con games and other forms of organized crime, he weeds out corrupt cops, judges, and politicians. Judges, congressmen, and state senators are arrested. Without the cooperation of the authorities, many con men are forced to go out of business.

1980s Joe Hynes—future Brooklyn, New York, District Attorney—becomes New York State's first medical fraud investigator.

1983 Posing as a "Dr. Fischer," con artist Konrad Kujau sells diaries he claims were written by Adolf Hitler to a German magazine for 10 million marks. Two million copies of the diaries are printed before German forgery experts determine they are fake—and not even very good fakes. Kujau is arrested and spends three years in prison.

1995 Con artist John Vogel is arrested after a life of living (and scamming) on the road, with his daughter, Jennifer, at his side. She later wrote the book *Flim-Flam Man: The True Story of My Father's Counterfeit Life*, in which she shared her father's advice: "Do unto others before they do unto you." Jennifer gives up on becoming a traveling con artist following her father's arrest for printing $20 million in counterfeit bills, the Secret Service's fourth-largest seizure of counterfeit money. Vogel escapes and later commits suicide after a botched bank robbery.[2]

2002 Steven Spielberg's movie *Catch Me if You Can* is released. The film stars Leonardo DiCaprio as Frank Abagnale Jr., probably the most famous impostor in recent history.

2004 Mother and son grifter team Sante and Kenneth Kimes are convicted of two murders, bringing to an end a long career as traveling flim-flammers.

Endnotes

Introduction
1. David W. Maurer, *The Big Con: The Story of the Confidence Man* (New York: Anchor Books, 1999), 2.
2. Patricia H. Holmes, "Con Artists and the Games They Play," Ohio State University Extension, Preble County, and Terri Tallman, Ohio District 5, Area Agency on Aging, 2005. http://www.ohioline.osu.edu/ss-fact/0154.html. Accessed April 11, 2008.
3. Ibid.
4. Ibid.
5. Lynn Riggs and Oscar Hammerstein II, *Oklahoma!*, screenplay to motion picture released by RKO Radio Pictures, 1955.
6. W.C. Fields and Everett Freeman, *You Can't Cheat an Honest Man*, from screenplay to motion picture released by Universal in 1939.

Chapter 1
1. Maurer, 299.
2. Selwyn Raab, *Five Families* (New York: St. Martin's Press, 2006), 215.
3. Ibid., 216.
4. David McKie, "The fall of a Midas," *The Guardian* Online, http://www.guardian.co.uk/Columnists/Column/0,5673,1136841,00.html. Posted on February 2, 2004.
5. BBC, "Hustle," http://www.bbc.co.uk/drama/hustle/. Accessed April 15, 2008.
6. Scripophily.net, "Denver City Consolidated Silver Mining Co. 1881 - Leadville, Colorado signed by J. Whitaker Wright," http://www.scripophily.net/dencitconsil1.html.
7. Richard Perez-Pena, "3-Card Monte: It's Just a Shell Game, Officials Warn," http://query.nytimes.com/gst/fullpage.html?res=9E0CE7D71131F932A25752C1A964958260. Posted on November 11, 1992.
8. Personal interview with New Jersey-native Michael Caracciolo, November 14, 2006.

Chapter 2
1. Edgar Allan Poe, *Complete Stories and Poems of Edgar Allan Poe* (New York: Doubleday, 1984); and Burton R. Pollin, "Poe's 'Diddling': Source of Title and Tale," *Southern Literary Review* (Fall 1969): 106–111.
2. "How Con Artists Set Up Their Victims," Fraud Aid, http://www.fraudaid.com/how_con_artists_set_up_

victim02.htm. Accessed April 11, 2008

Chapter 3

1. Mark Bulliet and Kieran Crowley, "Bogus badge fooled entire community," *New York Post*, February 8, 2007.
2. Ibid.
3. Ibid.
4. Ibid.
5. Tatiana Deligiannakis, "Collector taken for 600G in art of the steal," *New York Post*, July 19, 2006.
6. Ibid.
7. Laura Italiano, "Degas-Dancer Thief Pliés Guilty," http://www.nypost.com/seven/02062007/news/regionalnews/degas_dancer_thief_pli_s_guilty_regionalnews_laura_italiano.htm. Posted on February 6, 2007.
8. "It's death for ant-brain," *Daily News*, February 16, 2007.
9. Ibid.
10. Kati Cornell, "Con man: I preyed on priests," *New York Post*, January 25, 2007.
11. Ibid.
12. Laura Pulfer, "Frank Abagnale Jr.: Felon tells moral of his story," *Cincinnati Enquirer*, February 27, 2003.
13. Ibid.

Chapter 4

1. "False Reward Tricks," http://www.answers.com/topic/confidence-trick. Accessed April 11, 2008.
2. NBC4.com, "Money," http://www.nbc4.com/money/10753236/detail.html. Posted January 12, 2007.
3. Lore Croghan, "Internet scams trip lovelorn: Bride-seekers lose thousands," *Daily News*, June 30, 2006.
4. Ibid.
5. Press release, Patricia H. Holmes, "Con Artists and the Games They Play," Ohio State University Extension, Preble County, and Terri Tallman, Ohio District 5, Area Agency on Aging, 2005.
6. *Dateline NBC*, broadcast October 11, 2002.
7. Ibid.
8. "Interview with Madelyn Toogood," *CNN American Morning with Paula Zahn*, aired September 23, 2002. Transcript available at http://transcripts.cnn.com/TRANSCRIPTS/0209/23/ltm.07.html. Accessed April 11, 2008.
9. Ibid.
10. "Common Fraud Schemes," FBI Official Web Site, http://www.fbi.gov/majcases/fraud/fraudschemes.htm. Accessed April 11, 2008.
11. Holmes.
12. "Common Fraud Schemes."
13. Holmes.
14. "Common Fraud Schemes."
15. Maurer, 285.
16. Ibid., 291.
17. Ibid., 262–263.
18. Ibid., 292.
19. Ibid., 291.

Endnotes

Chapter 5
1. Michael Benson, *The Complete Idiot's Guide to National Security* (New York: Alpha Books, 2003), 243.
2. Julian E. Barnes, "Defense Sees Rush to Judge in Arrest of Mother and Son," *New York Times*, February 16, 2000.
3. Lisa Sweetingham, "Kenneth Kimes tells jurors his mother put him up to murder," CourtTV Online. http://www.courttv.com/trials/kimes/061704_ctv.html. Updated June 18, 2004.
4. Benson, *National Security*, 243.
5. Press release, "Utility Consumers' Action Network/Privacy Rights Clearinghouse and CALPIRG Charitable Trust," Released January 1997. Revised November 2002.
6. Ibid.
7. Ibid.
8. Benson, *National Security*, 243.
9. Ibid., 246.

Chapter 6
1. BBC News, "Fake bank website cons victims," http://news.bbc.co.uk/2/hi/technology/2308887.stm. Posted on October 8, 2002.
2. "An Old Swindle Revisited," *New York Times*, March 20, 1898, p. 12; and Arthur Train, "The Spanish Prisoner," *Cosmopolitan Magazine*, March 1910.
3. Ibid.
4. "Mamet," Filmmakers.com, http://www.filmmakers.com/artists/mamet/biography.
5. BBC News.
6. Ibid.
7. FTC Consumer Alert, "How Not to Get Hooked by a 'Phishing' Scam," Federal Trade Commission, http://www.ftc.gov/bcp/edu/pubs/consumer/alerts/alt127.shtm. Posted on October 2006.
8. Brian Bergstein, "Internet con artists turn to 'vishing'," *USA Today* Online, http://www.usatoday.com/tech/news/internetprivacy/2006-07-12-vishing-scam_x.htm. Posted on July 12, 2006.
9. Ibid.
10. Ibid.
11. Ibid.
12. Unsolicited e-mail (spam) sent to author on October 16, 2006.
13. Chris E. McGoey, "Scams and Con Games: How to Identify and Avoid Scams," Crime Doctor, http://www.crimedoctor.com/scams-con-games.htm. Accessed April 11, 2008.
14. Ibid.
15. Ibid.
16. "Federal Bureau of Investigation 2006 Financial Crime Report," http://www.fbi.gov/publications/financial/fcs_report2006/financial_crime_2006.htm. Accessed April 11, 2008.
17. "Undercover cop helps bust eBay scam," http://auctionscams.blogspot.com/2007/10/

undercover-cop-helps-bust-ebay-scam-uk.html. Posted on October 17, 2007.

Chapter 7
1. Maurer, 215–217.
2. Heidi Evans, "Call him King con! But slippery city hustler finally faces big squeeze," *Daily News*, December 31, 2006.
3. "Accused 9/11 gay con man arrested," *The Advocate*, http://findarticles.com/p/articles/mi_m1589/is_2003_July_22/ai_109270105. Posted on July 22, 2003.
4. Tom Shine, "Tall Tales of 9/11 Fraud," http://abcnews.go.c om/US/story?id=2183522&page=1. Posted on July 12, 2006.
5. Edward Wyatt, "More Arrests Made In 9/11 Fraud Cases," http://query.nytimes.com/gst/fullpage.html?res=940CE4D6173BF932A25757C0A9659C8B63&scp=1&sq=More+Arrests+Made+In+9%2F11+Fraud+Cases&st=nyt. Posted on April 11, 2003.
6. Evans.

Chapter 8
1. Federal Bureau of Investigation, "International Task Force Warns Consumers Not to Fall for Cross Border Lottery and Advance-Fee Scams," Press release, July 19, 2006. Official Web Site of the FBI, http://losangeles.fbi.gov/pressrel/2006/la071906.htm. Accessed April 11, 2008.
2. Ibid.
3. Ibid.
4. "International Task Force Warns…"
5. William F. Crowley, "A New Weapon Against Confidence Games," *The Journal of Criminal Law, Criminology, and Police Science* 50, 3 (September-October 1959): 233–236.
6. "Nicholas J. Johnson: Australia's Honest Con Man," http://www.conman.com.au. Accessed April 11, 2008.
7. Carl Campanile, "Bid to Finger Fraud: Medicaid 'prints'," *New York Post*, January 29, 2007.

Chapter 9
1. *Con Men: Fascinating Profiles of Swindlers and Rogues from the Files of the Most Successful Broadcast in Television History, 60 Minutes Classics* (New York: Simon & Schuster, 2003), 5.
2. Ibid., 7.
3. Ibid., 32.
4. Ibid., 50.
5. Ibid., 54.
6. Ibid., 188; and "Crooks and Con Men: The Best Moments and Most Unforgettable Characters," CBS News, http://www.cbsnews.com/stories/2004/01/16/60minutes/main593658.shtml?source=search_story. Accessed April 11, 2008.

Chronology

1. Leonard Maltin, *Leonard Maltin's 2006 Movie Guide* (New York: Penguin, 2006), 888.

2. Jennifer Vogel, *Flim-Flam Man: The True Story of My Father's Counterfeit Life* (New York: Simon & Schuster, 2005).

Glossary

bait and switch Occurs when a store advertises a sale to attract customers, who, once they're in, are charged regular or slightly higher prices instead of the promised discount.

blow To allow a victim to win some money in order to draw him further into the scam, sometimes called "the convincer."

bobble To make a mistake while committing a con, thus making the victim suspicious that something is up.

boodle A wad of fake money, used to replace real money during a con.

bunco A swindle, also used in *bunco squad* to describe police fraud departments; from the name of an oft-fixed gambling game.

button A set-up whereby a fake cop arrests the con artist and allows the mark to talk his way out of it, leaving the con man with the money and the mark feeling lucky for not being arrested.

ducats Card scam in which the mark is convinced he is in on the fix.

fit the mitt Bribe an official.

fix Successful bribe of the police, judges, juries, and elected officials.

grift Any criminal racket.

grifter Generally, a thief who moves from place to place, being clever, stealing without violence.

inside man The con artist's partner, whom the mark thinks is a stranger, otherwise known as a shill.

job As in "do the job," to lose on purpose. One who does the job is called a jobber.

kayfabe Coded language that con artists use in front of their marks.

lay the flue To switch fake money for real currency.

mark A con artist's intended victim, sometimes referred to as Mr. Bates.

rag Scam involving the stock market.

tat Short con game played with fixed dice.

tip A fixed poker game.

Bibliography

Benson, Michael. *The Complete Idiot's Guide to National Security*. New York: Alpha Books, 2003.

Bergstein, Brian. "Internet con artists turn to 'vishing'," *USA Today* Online. Available online. URL: http://www.usatoday.com. Posted on July 12, 2006.

Bertrand, Marsha. *Fraud!: How to Protect Yourself from Schemes, Scams, and Swindles*. New York: American Management Association, 1999.

Bulliet, Mark, and Kieran Crowley. "Bogus badge fooled entire community." *New York Post*, February 8, 2007.

Campanile, Carl. "Bid to Finger Fraud: Medicaid 'prints'." *New York Post*, January 29, 2007.

Cornell, Kati. "Con man: I preyed on priests." *New York Post*, January 25, 2007.

Croghan, Lore. "Internet scams trip lovelorn: Bride-seekers lose thousands." *Daily News*, June 30, 2006.

"Crooks and Con Men: The Best Moments and Most Unforgettable Characters," CBS News. Available online. URL: http://www.cbsnews.com.

Crowley, William F. "A New Weapon Against Confidence Games," *The Journal of Criminal Law, Criminology, and Police Science* 50, 3 (September–October 1959): 233–236.

Deligiannakis, Tatiana. "Collector taken for 600G in art of the steal." *New York Post*, July 19, 2006.

Evans, Heidi. "Call him King con! But slippery city hustler finally faces big squeeze." *Daily News*, December 31, 2006.

"Fake bank website cons victims," BBC News. Available online. URL: http://www.news.bbc.co.uk.

"How Con Artists Set Up Their Victims," Fraud Aid. Available online. URL: http://fraudaid.com.

"International Task Force Warns Consumers Not to Fall for Cross Border Lottery and Advance-Fee Scams," FBI official Web site. Available online. URL: http://www.fbi.gov.

"It's death for ant-brain." *Daily News*, February 16, 2007.

Lueck, Thomas J. "Murderer Reveals New Details In Slaying of Socialite in 1998," *New York Times* Online. Available online. URL: http://www.nytimes.com.

Maltin, Leonard. *Leonard Maltin's 2006 Movie Guide.* New York: Penguin, 2006.

"Mamet," Filmmakers.com. Available online. URL: http://www.filmmakers.com/artists/mamet/biography.

Maurer, David W. *The Big Con: The Story of the Confidence Man.* New York: Anchor Books, 1999.

McKie, David. "The fall of a Midas," *The Guardian* Online. Available online. URL: http://www.guardian.co.uk.

Mott, Graham M. *Scams, Swindles, and Rip-Offs.* Littleton, Colo.: Golden Shadows Press, 1994.

Poe, Edgar Allan. *Complete Stories and Poems of Edgar Allan Poe.* New York: Doubleday, 1984.

Pollin, Burton R. "Poe's 'Diddling': Source of Title and Tale," *Southern Literary Review* (Fall 1969): 106–111.

Raab, Selwyn. *Five Families.* New York: Thomas Dunne Books, 2006.

The Silver Lake Editors. *Scams & Swindles.* Lansdowne, Penn.: Silver Lake Publishing, 2006.

Sweetingham, Lisa. "Kenneth Kimes tells jurors his mother put him up to murder," CourtTV Online. Available online. URL: http://www.courttv.com.

Train, Arthur. "The Spanish Prisoner," *Cosmopolitan Magazine*, March 1910.

You Can't Cheat an Honest Man. Universal Studios, 1939.

Further Resources

Books

Asbury, Herbert. *Sucker's Progress: An Informal History of Gambling in America.* New York: Thunder Mouth Press, 2005.

Con Men: Fascinating Profiles of Swindlers and Rogues from the Files of the Most Successful Broadcast in Television History, 60 Minutes Classics. New York: Simon & Schuster, 2003.

Vogel, Jennifer. *Flim-Flam Man: The True Story of My Father's Counterfeit Life.* New York: Simon & Schuster, 2005.

Web Sites

McGoey, Chris E. "Scams and Con Games: How to Identify and Avoid Scams," Crime Doctor.
http://www.crimedoctor.com

Index

Page numbers in *italics* indicate images.

A
Abagnale, Frank, Jr. *41*, 42, 96
acting skills, of con artists 35
Adair, Donald 76
address, fraudulent use of 61
advance-fee con 63–66, *64*, 80
affidavits, on ID theft 60
Albania, pyramid scheme in 88–89, *89*
Alexander, Norman 39–40
American Red Cross, as victim of cons 75, *76*
ant con, in China 40
art cons 39–40
ATM card, theft of 60

B
bait and switch 44
banco 17
bank examiner scam 44
Better Business Bureau 44, 45
Bible 10
big cons 24–27
"The Big Mitt" 52
big store 24
Blakey, G. Robert 20
Blay-Miezah, John Ackah 93–94
blood analysis 10
"the blow" 31
blowing off the mark 33
bobble 30
boodles 55
Boris and Natasha schemes 45–46
Bradley, Ed 93–94
breakdown 31
bribes
    for law enforcement officials 20, 73–74, *74*
    for police impersonator 37
Brooklyn Bridge 49, *50*
Bullwinkle (cartoon) 46
bunco 16–17, 82
bunco squad 16–18, 95
button 21

C
Cain and Abel 10
card games 52–55
    banco 17
    "The Big Mitt" 52
    ducats 52
    Find the Lady 23
    Three-Card Monte 23
    tip (fixed poker) 52–55
carneys 33
carnival cons 33, 82
Case of the Lottery Ticket Losers 49
Catch Me If You Can (movie) *41*, *42*, *96*
Catholic Church, as victim of con 40–42
charity cons 45
checks, theft of 60
Chinese con 40
chronology of cons 95–96
churches, as victim of con 40–42
clean carpet caper 44
computer cons 63–72
    advance-fee (419) con 63–66, *64*
    identity theft 61–62
    phishing and spam 66–71, *67*
    reporting 80
    Web site impostors 71–72
computer viruses 67
con(s). *See also specific types*
    anatomy of 29–34
    big or long 24–27, *32*
    chronology of 95–96
    common 43–55
    as fraud 16

106

Index

as magic/show business 82–83
media investigations of 87–94
protection against 16, 79–85
public education on 17–18, 79–85
short 21–24, *22*
tactics for combating 54
violence in 58–59
con artists 15
confidence 22
confidence men or women 15
con job 29
conscience, lack of 73–78
contest con 46–49
contracts, as con 51
"convincer" 31
counterfeit cons 55, 88
credit card theft 57–61
credit reports 57
crime 9–11
 biblical 10
 effects of 9
Crotty, Paul 78
Cuomo, Andrew 84

D

Daniel (biblical figure) 10
DiCaprio, Leonardo 42, 96
dice games *53*, 55
 bunco 16–17, 82
 "Electric Bar" 55
 tat 23–24
diddling 30
doctors, impersonation of 35
door-to-door salesmen 51
Doyle, Thomas 39–40
driver's license, identity theft and 61
ducats 52

E

eBay, cons via 67–68, 71–72
e-cons 63–72
 advance-fee (419) con 63–66, *64*
 identity theft 61–62
 phishing and spam 66–71, *67*
 reporting 80
 Web site impostors 71–72
education, about cons 17–18, 79–85

"Electric Bar" 55
eluding justice 73–74
e-mail 63–72. *See also* e-cons
embarrassment, of mark 15–16, 21
emotional manipulation 75–78
emotional pleas 51–52
Equifax 57
ethnic groups, as con artists *47*, 47–48
Experian 57

F

Federal Bureau of Investigation (FBI) 79–80, 96
Federal Emergency Management Agency, con of 76
Federal Trade Commission (FTC) 66, 80
"fiddle game" 43–44
Fields, W.C. 18, 95
films 18, 20, 35, *41*, 42, 93
Find the Lady 23
fingerprinting
 history of 10
 of Medicare recipients 84–85, *85*
firefighters, impersonation of 35
fit the mitt 73
fix, putting in 33–34, 73–74
fixer 74
Flim-Flam Man: The True Story of My Father's Counterfeit Life (Vogel) 96
flue, laying the 55
419 con 63–66, *64*, 80
fraud. *See also specific types*
 con games as 16
Fredericks, Scott 75–78
fun, cons for 38

G

gambling cons 16–17, 52–55, 80–82
Georgia Boys 48
Gere, Richard 93
giving the breakdown 31
giving the convincer 31
greed, of mark 19
grifters 15, 35

H

hackers 61–62
health care fraud 49–50, 75–78, 83, 84–85, *85*
"Help Needed" scam 51
Henn, Patric 75
Henry, Paul 68
Hitler, Adolf, fake diary of 89–90, *90*, 96
Hoax (movie) 93
Holmes, Patricia H. 16, 51
Honest Con Man 82
House of Games (movie) 65
Hughes, Howard, fake autobiography of 93, 95
Hurricane Katrina con 76
Hustle (television show) 20
Hynes, Joe 84–85, 96

I

identity (ID) theft 57–62
    scope of 61–62
    victims' guide on 57–61
illness, feigning 75–78
impersonation 35–39, *36*
informant 17, 54
inside men 21
inspector scams 46
insurance fraud, medical 83, 84–85, *85*
international efforts, against cons 79–80
Internet Crime Complaint Center 80
Internet scams 63–72
    advance-fee (419) con 63–66, *64*
    identity theft 61–62
    phishing and spam 66–71, *67*
    reporting 80
    Web site impostors 71–72
investigations
    inter-agency, success story of 80–82
    international 79–80
    media 87–94
Irish Travellers *47*, 47–48
Irving, Clifford *92*, 93, 95

J

job, con 29
Johnson, Nicholas J. 82–83
journalism, investigative 87–94
justice, eluding 73–74

K

Katrina, Hurricane, con 76
kayfabe 33, 95
Kazdin, David 58–59
Kimes, Kenneth *58*, 58–59, 96
Kimes, Sante 58–59, *59*, 96
Kroft, Steve 87–88
Kujau, Konrad 90, *90*, 96

L

law enforcement
    bribery of officials 20, 73–74, *74*
    bunco squad 16–18, 95
    characteristics of police officers 9
    eluding 73–74
    failure to contact 15–16, 20–21
    impersonators 35–39
    inter-agency, success story of 80–82
    international efforts 79–80
    patience in 9–10
    tactics for combating cons 54
    tools used in 10–11
laying the flue 55
literary scams 89–93
Little Caesar (movie) 20
lonely hearts scam 45–46
long cons 24–27, *32*
lottery ticket cons 49

M

Mafia 15
magazine subscription cons 49
magic, con games as 82–83
magnetized dice *53*, 55
Mamet, David 65
manipulation, emotional 75–78
mark
    becoming, tips on avoiding 79–80
    blowing off 33

Index

"convincer" for 31
embarrassment of 15–16, 21
greed of 19
"putting up" (selecting) 29
roping 29–30
silencing of 20–21
McNish, Carlton 75
media investigations 87–94
medical cons 49–50, 75–78, 83, 84–85, *85*
medical degrees, counterfeit 88
Medicare cons, protection against 84–85, *85*
mining con 20, 95
Mississippi Travellers 48
mobsters 15
mole (undercover agent) 17
money
con and fraud gains 15
counterfeit 55
as object of crime 15
rules for dealing with 16
taking off the touch 32
"money box" scam 19
Morgenthau, Robert M. 75
movies 18, 20, 35, *41*, 42, 93
The Music Man (musical and movie) 35, 95

N

National Criminal Intelligence Service (NCIS, United Kingdom) 63–66
Newman, Paul 25, *25*
New York Times 87
Nigeria, advance-fee con from 63–66, *64*
9/11 cons 75
nomadic groups *47*, 47–48
"nonprofit" cons 45

O

O'Brien, Ron 68
odometer scam 87–88
old man-young man team 38
Oman-Ghana fund 93–94
Osakwe, Obum *64*
Otukoya, Olamrewaju 72
Otukoya, Temitope 72

P

passports, identity theft and 61
patience
in con game 31
in law enforcement 9–10
PayPal con 67–68
petting zoo con 80–82
phishing 66–71, *67*
PhoneBusters 80
phone cons 49–50, 68, 80
"pigeon-drop" con 51
playing the con 29–30
Poe, Edgar Allan 30
poker, fixed games 52–55
police officers
bribery of 20, 73–74, *74*
bunco squad 16–18, 95
characteristics of 9
eluding 73–74
failure to contact 15–16, 20–21
impersonation of 35–39, *36*
tactics for combating cons 54
tools used by 10–11
Ponzi, Charles 91, *91*
Ponzi scheme 91
postal address, fraudulent use of 61
priests
impersonation of 35
as victims of con 40–42
Privacy Rights Clearinghouse 60
protection against cons 16, 79–85
public education, on cons 17–18, 79–85
putting in the fix 33–34, 73–74
"putting the mark up" 29
pyramid scheme
Albania as victim of 88–89, *89*
explanation of 88

R

Racketeer Influenced and Corrupt Organizations (RICO) Act 19–20, 95
rag 24–27
real estate cons 49–50
Redford, Robert 25, *25*
reporting cons 57–61, 80
RICO laws 19–20, 95

Riggio, Robert 40–42
Rodin sculpture, theft of 39–40
roper 23
roping the mark 29–30
Rosen, Steven 48
Royal Canadian Mounted Police (RCMP) 79–80
Russian women con 45–46

S
Sawyer, Diane 88
Scam (Wright) 48
Schmidt, Howard 62
September 11 cons 75
settings, phony 24–27, 25, 31, 32
shame, lack of 73–78
Shaw, Robert 25
shell game 21–23, 22
shills 21, 23
"short-changing" 21
short cons 21–24, 22
show business, con artists in 82–83
Silverman, Irene 58–59
silver mine con 20, 95
60 Minutes 87–94
sleight of hand 51–52, 82–83
Social Security numbers 60–61
sociopaths, con artists as 73
spam scam 66–71, 67
The Spanish Prisoner (movie) 65
"Spanish prisoner" con 65
Spielberg, Steven 42, 96
spoof sites 71–72
The Sting (movie) 25, 25
stock market con 24–27
subscription cons 49

T
taking off the touch 32
tat (dice game) 23–24
telephone cons 49–50, 68, 80
telling the tale 30–31
Terry, Henry 35–39, 36
Three-Card Monte 23
tip (fixed card game) 52–55

tip, in stock market con 26
Toogood, Madelyne 47, 48
TransUnion 57
"Travel Club Trick" 51–52
20/20 87
two-man team 38

U
undercover agent 17, 54
United States Postal Service 61
"Unknown Caller" scam 52
U.S.-Canadian task force 79–80

V
victim. *See* mark
violence, in cons 58–59
viruses, computer 67
vishing 68
Vogel, Jennifer 96
Vogel, John 96
Voice over Internet Protocol (VoIP) 68
voice phishing 68

W
Wang Zhendong 40
Washington Post 87
Web site impostors 71–72
Webster, William H. 96
weighted dice 53
West Africa, advance-fee con from 63–66, 64
Whitlow, Bill 87–88
Wilson, Meredith 95
winners, in contest con 46–49
World Trade Center fraud 75
wrestling, pro 33
Wright, Don 48
Wright, James Whitaker 20, 95
Wright, James Whitaker, III 20

Y
You Can't Cheat an Honest Man (movie) 18, 95
young man-old man team 38

About the Author

Michael Benson is the author or co-author of 41 books, including the true-crime books *Betrayal in Blood*, *Lethal Embrace*, and *Hooked Up For Murder*. He's also written *The Encyclopedia of the JFK Assassination* and Complete Idiot's Guides to NASA, National Security, The CIA, Submarines, and Modern China. Other works include biographies of Ronald Reagan, Bill Clinton, and William Howard Taft. Originally from Rochester, N.Y., he is a graduate of Hofstra University.

About the Consulting Editor

John L. French is a 31-year veteran of the Baltimore City Police Crime Laboratory. He is currently a crime laboratory supervisor. His responsibilities include responding to crime scenes, overseeing the preservation and collection of evidence, and training crime scene technicians. He has been actively involved in writing the operating procedures and technical manual for his unit and has conducted training in numerous areas of crime scene investigation. In addition to his crime scene work, Mr. French is also a published author, specializing in crime fiction. His short stories have appeared in *Alfred Hitchcock's Mystery Magazine* and numerous anthologies.